Soon

Tales from Hospice

Also by A. G. Mojtabai

Soon

Tales from Hospice

A. G. Mojtabai

Z

ZOLAND BOOKS
Cambridge, Massachusetts

First edition published in 1998 by
Zoland Books, Inc.
384 Huron Avenue
Cambridge, Massachusetts 02138

Copyright © 1998 by A. G. Mojtabai

Excerpts from *The Juniper Tree and Other Tales from Grimm*
translated by Lore Segal and Randall Jarrell with pictures by
Maurice Sendak. Translation copyright © 1973 by Lore Segal.
Pictures copyright © 1973 by Maurice Sendak. Reprinted by
permission of Farrar, Straus & Giroux, Inc.

The epigraph in "Nola" is from "Sacraments: Enter the
World of God's Imagination," by Alex Garcia-Rivera,
U.S. Catholic, January 1994, p. 7.

FIRST EDITION

Book design by Boskydell Studio
Printed in the United States of America

05 04 03 02 01 00 99 98   8 7 6 5 4 3 2 1

This book is printed on acid-free paper, and its binding
materials have been chosen for strength and durability.

Library of Congress Cataloging-in-Publication Data
Mojtabai, A. G., 1937–
Soon: : tales from hospice / A.G. Mojtabai. —1st ed.
p. cm.
ISBN 0-944072-91-7
1. Hospices (Terminal care)—Fiction. 2. Terminally ill—Fiction.
3. Hospice care—Fiction. I. Title.
PS3563.0374S58 1998
813'.54—dc21   98-29015
                                                          CIP

REMEMBERING

John Tully Carmody

1939–1995,

FRIEND AND INQUISITOR,

GREATLY MISSED

"Last Things" and "Wedding" were originally published in *Nimrod*, "Long Distance" in *Hospice*, "The Juniper Tree" in *Fiction*, "Isolation" in *The Antioch Review*, and "Nola" in *Shenandoah*.

I live in weird equipose, all the time now,
like a banded turkey, one foot on top of the other,
my heart jumping between two weights.

— Gerald Stern, *Rejoicings*

Contents

CONTENTS ✦ X

Preface

FOR YEARS, coming upon St. Anthony's Hospital in Amarillo, Texas, I'd stare at the covered crossway connecting — and separating — hospital and hospice. What would that crossing be like? I wondered, for, to me, it loomed overhead like the bridge to another world. I'd strain my eyes trying to make out what I could through the tinted windows on the ground floor of the hospice building — very little, as I learned later, and not at all what I'd thought. Those shadowy passing figures in what turned out to be a common room were most likely relatives of a patient, or volunteers tidying up. The doubly mysterious windows on the second floor, through which nothing at all could be seen, marked administrative offices. For years, I spooked myself with conjectures before I summoned up the nerve to actually enter the building and face down my fears.

My entrance scene was played out some years ago, and only through a concerted effort of memory and imagination have I been able to recapture it. I would not trouble others to pass through that door with me unless I believed that those ancient fears of mine were widely shared.

After three months of training and many more months on

the ward, the stories started coming. I was not privy to family histories, or medical histories, so I was forced to invent. All I had were glimpses. The opening episodes are literally that: glimpses. I noticed a woman in a turban, sitting up in bed, writing one letter after another. What was in them? I had to write those letters myself in order to find out; they are brought together in "Last Things." "Soon" was another glimpse: of a woman combing her mother's hair. Not much talking going on there. I tried to fill their silence with the words they couldn't say. Then, in the course of my rounds, I was struck by the sight of a woman with an orchid pinned to her pillow. I wanted to know why the orchid had been placed there. No one could tell me, so I wrote the story "Nola" to explain it. The sight of an emaciated man in a plaid bathrobe, walking down the corridor, using his IV pole for support, conjoined with my reading of cancer diaries, set me to the writing of "Zone." A fragment of speech — a patient's voice telling me to "hurry!" — still reverberates in my memory: I tried to capture one possible version of that echo in "The Juniper Tree," where it becomes the last word of a dying child. . . . The stories kept on coming.

Although I chose to set the book in a ward (an inpatient unit conferring at least a minimal unity of time and place on otherwise disparate tales of different and very separate lives), I must remind the reader that hospice is as much a mode of practice as a place. Much — indeed, most — hospice care is carried on in patients' homes. Yet I continue to think of hospice in both senses, as a practice and a place, for the term *hospice,* linked to *hospital* and *hostel,* derived from the Latin *hospitium,* was traditionally used to refer to a place of shelter, a place of rest, for pilgrims and travelers, well or infirm — wayfarers all, on a perilous, marvelous journey. The hospice I'm writing about is such a place.

Hospice (practice and place) is about hospitality to strangers. And from this hospitality comes, every now and then, a sort of healing. No stones rolled away or tombs vacated — I don't mean that. Entering a patient's room, I'm always aware of how little I, or anyone, can do. Almost nothing: a cool washcloth applied, a bedpan emptied, a telephone receiver held to the ear, a fresh sheet, a listening presence, a quick retreat where indicated, a hand and voice remaining in the time, so starkly illumined, after the Sacrament of Anointing is completed. Help comes when it will, through a mutual unfolding. And, happening to be present at a graced moment, sometimes I am startled to find — *this* side of death — the old barriers rolled away, stranger turning towards stranger with no other strangeness than the ease of the turning.

Those moments have given me the courage to presume.

I

Looking On

Last Things

A QUIET DAY. It occurs to Helen that it's Thursday — her usual day for the hairdresser back in the days when she had usual days. That was once upon a time, yet not so long ago.

Her bed is tilted all the way up, and, braced by it, Helen sits forward, unslumped, readying a supply of pens and a box of notepaper on the tray table. She's wearing a silky, powder blue bed jacket and a terry-cloth turban of the same pale hue, still keeping up appearances, trying to. Pausing in her preparations, she fingers musingly the plastic medical bracelets. They're both on her left wrist, she notices. She never paid attention when the bracelets were being strapped on. Left wrist . . . heart side — is that why? Or is it because left's the side nearest the door, to save the staff time? The blue bracelet came first, then the yellow; the different colors have different meanings, she's afraid to ask what. She tries not to glance at the catheter bag, like a purse with a clear plastic front, hitched low to the side rail of the bed, to the fluid displayed in it — her own — the color of medium-dark tea. Helen does her best not to dwell on things like this, for she has work to do.

She draws the table closer. Plucks a sheet of notepaper out of the box. The pen: stares at it as if she fully expects it to turn into a flowering branch. Almost laughs, then recollects. Takes two long, deep breaths with pursed lips, as she's been instructed to do. Then she arrows the pen at the notepaper where an ornamental border of trumpet vine crowds out much of the space. The reverse side, having no border, is roomier; she'll do most of her writing there. She's sorting out everything that pertains to keeping.

This is Helen's third visit to the inpatient unit. Her hope is to have her medications fine-tuned, the pain well under control, and go home again. Home for the duration, she has no illusions about that. She thinks of this period as her third reprieve. According to Medicare, she's entitled to only one more, the fourth is final.

She *could* fret about Medicare and such, but she'll cross that bridge when. *If* and when — it's not likely. But, right now, she has other things to do. They've got to be done. She'd best start out with the letter to Wayne.

Dear favorite nephew,

She reminds herself to get through the birthday greetings quickly, then right down to business. There's only so much energy she can count on —

> *. . . I'm leaving you the picture of your father, the one you always said you liked. Your father was a gentleman — don't believe a word otherwise. Hard to realize Tom won't be coming back. It's been a very tame two years since he's gone to his rest, altogether far too quiet without him. He wasn't perfect, no need to remind you of that. For better or worse money never stuck to his fingers. A little fondness for the bottle (true) and for the*

ladies (also) — the bubblies and the lovelies, as he called them. And for gabbing, Tom was a past master at that. He had the sweetest nature, bless his soul, the most lovely man, I weep to think of him yet. But enough — I won't keep you, I'm sure you're very busy and I, sad to say, am not.

A few more words to bring the business to a close, then the signature, with curlicues on the staffs of the *H* and a rising curve on the tail of the *n*, ending with a flourish. So there! She shifts the written page to the left side of the table.

One down. Not too difficult. The next one should be even easier — it's to her best friend.

Dearest Nova,

How are you, dear? You and Alice, bless your hearts, are the only ones who still write to me these days. How I wish you both lived closer. Can't ever have enough of wishing, can we? They say it's only to get the medications adjusted, but I know I'm only buying time. Quality time, I hope, as much quality as can be bought. The thing that's coming is sure in any case. So I want to let you know now that my black satin evening bag with the silver chain and the jet bead design you so admired is yours. A little something to hang on to when I'm gone —

By the way — the evening bag was given to me by my dear husband that rat two years before he walked out on me. I used it only once, so it's fresh as a baby's bottom. Feeling sort of strange today, why I'm writing this. You probably know the wadded-up feeling, the tiredness — feeling thrashed all over — that's familiar enough. Unfortunately! But this other thing is nothing I've ever felt before. No sensation in my toes except now and then a crawling, very distant. It's not painful, just strange. But enough of me.

Take care of yourself, good care. Now before I get soggy — Vaya con Dios, my dear friend,

My dear . . .

She signs her name, starting off with a flourish, ending without. Her breeziness is a pose, she's all too aware of the fact. Paper courage. Still — by dressing herself in the gestures, she hopes to feel what they pretend to show. And now — before her brave front sags — better keep on with it!

Moving along. . . . Another dear friend:

Dearest Alice,

Let's be shameless hussies — shall we? — flags flying to the end, and never go down faintly like ladies of "the finer sort." By all means, buy the swirly blue skirt with the daffodils on it. Suggest you add flounces. And don't forget the red shoes! If not now, when, dear?

So happens it's quiet at the moment, but soon the nurses will be creeping around for "vitals" — that's vital signs. By the way, what is this thing about "little"? Here the nurses say "the little lady" and "the dear little man," and I shudder. Let's not be little, ever!

A hint about what she's going to send to Alice, and she signs off. No frills or flourishes this time — she's budgeting the extras — but a clear, firm signature, at least.

Only two more to go. Can she hold out? She thinks she can, she hopes so. Right now it's sweltering under her turban. Helen casts a glance through the open door, into the gray space of the corridor, makes out some faint fussing noises in the distance, somewhere in the vicinity of the nurses' station, but nothing stirring in her particular neck of the woods. She lifts her turban to catch the breeze, then, still feeling hot and prickly, removes it altogether, stowing it on her lap, close to hand. Running a hand over her scalp is like touching new-mown grass, nothing like the texture of hair. While she's at it, she extricates one arm from her bed jacket, then the other, then drags the nuisance free, tossing it to the foot end of the bed. She's amazed at how much of an exertion this is, but she's not undone yet. It's a whole lot cooler now, to be sure. Best get back to the letter writing, as long as her strength permits.

To Henry, another nephew — she's decided on the olive-wood coffee table. A few words of explanation to start, only by the greatest kindness not mentioning how much Henry had irked her by putting his feet up on it, without taking off his shoes as Helen requested. Its surface is still smooth, though, despite Henry. Swiftly concluding the business part of her letter, she can't resist a few more words.

This may be the last you hear from me on "terra firma," as they say. Let me assure you that it's far from firm. A word to the wise, my dear, while there's still time. Yesterday, I was feeling better and thought I might just surprise everybody by deciding to live. Would I, if I could? You betcha! I'd like to live so long I'd have to be carried around in a basket. Today I think I'll pass. Feel like I've been trying to thread the point end of a needle all day long. Believe me — that's tired out.

The letter comes to an abrupt halt with a wavering "Take care." Her hand is trembling — she has to print her name.

Only one more. She doesn't think she can make it, but she has to try. She puts down the pen a moment and gently rubs her writing arm, wrist, and fingers, to get the feeling back. Raising her arm, she stares at it. So wasted: the flesh drapes from the bone. Her skin has the curious feel of some expensive fabric whose name escapes her. Some kind of brocaded . . . Or, no, looser — crepe de chine, is it? Not sure. She feels her own skin from the outside, that's what's so strange.

Her bed is a raft, littered with get-well cards, snippets of floral ribbon, the leftover saltiness from the lunch she couldn't eat, her turban, and the pretty pink foam swabs that do for toothbrushes now that her gums are so tender. One second, she's looking down at the pink swabs, and the next her head's starting to nod, she's almost adrift . . . But only for a second! She snaps upright — back in time to catch the pen before it leaps —

She writes even more rapidly this time, her words starting to run together.

Dear Julie — You of course as my only daughter are to get everything I've left — dining room set, the singing crystal, cut glass, black walnut breakfront, grandfather clock, beds and night tables, loveseat, rugs and I forget. It's all spelled out with my lawyer Darryl Williams that lovely man in Corpus. You have the address the phone number I know I sent it. And there's a copy in the safety. Just a few other things to go to some other dear ones you'll find out about by and by . . .

A little more in this vein, the letters tottering, slanting now right, now left, swaying —

Signing this last letter, steadying her right hand with her left, Helen is relieved to see that she's accomplished what she set out to do. All but the addresses. Julie can finish up on those if she — Helen, herself — is not able. She scoots the bed table down past her knees. For now, she's bone tired. Just enough strength, she calculates, to press the button that lowers the head of the bed. That's it. She sighs. Much, much better . . .

But a few minutes later she's restless again. She summons the energy, and it comes — from where she does not know — enough to raise the head of the bed and draw the tray table close once again. There's a hidden drawer in the table, and she opens that, extracting mirror and folding stand, not forgetting to angle the glass carefully so that it's centered on nose and lips, the upper rim framed by the eyebrows, nothing above the eyebrows. She extracts a tube of lipstick — Shalimar red — and, again carefully, as though drawing back the plunger of a syringe, uncaps it and expertly traces her signature of three strokes, amplifying the upper lip with two buds joined only a little to the right of midpoint. She reaches for a tissue, presses it twice to her lips to blot the excess. Then, without bothering to push the table away, she presses the button that eases her down. There! Not an instant too soon. She closes her eyes. She's all written out.

Soon

JAMIE'S MOTHER was sitting in one of the visitors' chairs. She was trying to recollect the recipe for a salad that made a full meal, an easy summer dish, good for Jamie to have on hand. "The eggs should be sliced thin — circles, not wedges," she said. "Then you add chives, red pepper, mushrooms, dill, olives, angels —"

Jamie, who'd been combing her mother's hair, halted in midstroke. "You must mean anchovies," she put in.

"That's what I said," her mother answered in a cutting tone. Her face had been tilted away from Jamie, towards the courtyard door, as though she were hearing something in that direction, but she turned now to face Jamie's chest and resumed her recipe. Jamie kept on combing, though more slowly than before. Her mother had always acted as though she had no idea how ill she was and clearly wasn't about to change her policy, not even now. This made conversation difficult.

Jamie's full name was Jamila Kerry Waters. Her mother had named her Jamila for someone she'd read about in a book, some book she'd read in her teens and long since forgotten. Jamie's friends and the rest of the family had never used the name, never liked it; the nickname Jamie really suited her better. She'd been a chunky, brown-haired girl, and now was a chunky, plain-looking woman, whose eyes, too closely set together and inclined to squint, gave her an intense, crossly scrutinizing expression — the look of a woman threading a needle. A stranger's first glance gravitated not to her face, though, but to the thickness of her calves, the squareness of her stomach and hips. In these and other respects she took after her father.

Her mother was an altogether different story: small, fine boned, delicately sculpted, with soulful eyes, long and lustrous black hair, even now, at the beginning of her sixties, coming in only a little gray at the temples and underneath, around the ears, where no one but her hairdresser, and now Jamie, would know about it. She still had the graceful carriage of the professional ballroom dancer she'd been. For a number of years, she'd been a champion, she and her partner the best in the state, and then in the tristate region. She'd deserted her family for dancing. Jamie, who'd been raised by her father and her father's mother, both strong Baptists, did not dance, and, while she did not share their view of dancing as sinful, she thought it foolishness, and couldn't imagine a grown person taking something so childish seriously.

Jamie despaired of her own hair. "A mop," she called it, "wild," always needing to be "managed." She'd just yesterday gotten a perm — her hair felt completely dried out; the curls were too tight and crinkly, exposing too much forehead. She told her husband that she'd regretted the perm the minute it was done; she felt like a peeled onion, if truth be told. Didn't seem to bother him any, though. All he would say about it was, "Sure got your nickel's worth this time." What made it even worse was the fact that it was *his* nickel — Steve's — but he had the grace not to rub it in. Only on the subject of Jamie's mother did he hold nothing back. He was afraid of the woman's influence, that Jamie "might get ideas."

A visitor passing down the hall and spotting the two women in the room together would find it hard to believe that they were indeed mother and daughter. Actually, it didn't require a stranger's point of view to see it this way; Jamie herself often thought of her mother as a distant aunt who'd surfaced only when it was too late to mean anything for anyone. Someone utterly selfish, who'd come back only when she was too helpless to live on her own. That had happened a couple years back, at the funeral of Jamie's father. In all fairness, though, Jamie had to remind herself that her father had been the one who'd forbidden her mother ever to visit.

"You owe her nothing," Jamie's husband insisted. "What did she ever do for you?"

When Steve started harping like this, Jamie tended not to answer, but, the first time he'd brought it up, she said exactly what came to her: "She gave me life."

That hadn't slowed Steve down for an instant. "Nine months — you've given it back," he said. "You've used it up already. How long's she been sick? Going on two and a half years? You've given it back with overtime."

Jamie had no good answer to this, and no answer at all, good or bad, to what Steve said next: "And how about your own kids?" he pressed.

Her own kids — both boys — were managing as well as anyone could hope for. They were a lot happier, in fact, when Jamie had something of her own to occupy herself with, and was off their backs to that extent. They were doing just fine. One was in the local junior college, his second year. The "baby" — Brad — was a senior in high school, busy with varsity basketball. The family only seemed to meet coming and going these days; it hardly mattered where Jamie spent the time in between.

From as far back as she could remember, Jamie had wanted a daughter, though Steve was perfectly satisfied with what they had. He said two children were all they could afford. But Jamie really had nothing to complain about, they were nice enough boys.

"Tell me if I'm hurting you," Jamie said. She continued combing as gently as she could. The monotony of her strokes made her almost dreamy. There were so many strands to this. . . . She worked at a snarl with her fingers, with no result, the snarl coming undone only when she was on the verge of giving up; then the knot loosened, and a thick spill of hair streamed over the back of Jamie's hand. Jamie closed her eyes to receive it. It felt so much like running water. . . . She could see clearly the tense spread of her own small fingers tangled in her mother's hair long long ago, trying to catch the same whispery fullness. Jamie couldn't help believing that she actually *remembered* this: the sensation was so sharp — real, even to her fingertips. And she couldn't help believing that her mother remembered as well, that she, too, often thought of it — even though it had never happened. Never could have happened, for Jamie was scarcely more than a month old when her mother had walked off for good.

Jamie opened her eyes and stared blindly at the comb in her hand.

How could any of this matter now? Everything would soon be over, as even Steve had to admit. Only Jamie's mother would not concede the fact. The social worker called it a case of the most stubborn denial. Where, Jamie wondered, did she think her big belly came from that she defended like a treasure,

waking and sleeping — those wasted arms? Not even her admission to hospice seemed to register. On good days, she acted
as if the two of them were guests in the house of a distinguished
friend. "It's been perfectly lovely — your having us," she once
said to a startled student nurse. Other days, she acted as if the
place were a hotel of some sort, a hotel of inferior quality. She
complained at least once a day about the "room service." Only
yesterday she'd asked Jamie to set her shoes outside the door
to be "taken care of" — meaning what? polished? — while she
slept. She was likely talking about the black pumps with the
crossed straps that she'd worn in her exhibition days, a pair
Jamie had never seen except in photographs. And she gave
Jamie instructions to "send down" to have her blue satin
cleaned and pressed. What blue satin? Down *where*? Jamie
didn't even bother to ask. They were on the ground floor. In
reality, her mother hadn't worn anything but a nightgown
and two faded housecoats for the past month. Her pink pile
bedroom slippers were shapeless, stretched out at the sides
where her feet had swollen. Sometimes even the slippers
were too much. Like today — she was wearing socks now,
plain white cotton socks. Her talk made no sense. Why would
there be all these get-well cards on the windowsill — a bed
with side rails — a wheelchair and a portable commode close
to the bed — if this were a hotel? What kind of hotel could
it be?

Sometimes her mother would say, "I feel so ugly," but Jamie
refused to dignify such a remark with a reply. It was simply another one of her games: her mother hadn't a clue as to what it
meant to be ugly.

It was hard to figure out how much her mother truly knew
or did not know, felt or did not feel. She acted as if she fully in-
tended to go out. Every morning, she painted up her face: pow-

der, rouge, lipstick. And eyeliner — elongating the lids to make her eyes look almond shaped, Oriental, exotic. Then a dab of perfume from a bottle of smoked glass, shaped like the breast of a small bird. It had a wing-shaped knob on the stopper, a Frenchy name. Her mother had pronounced the name of the perfume for her any number of times — an airy, chiming sound that came out tinny or whangy whenever Jamie tried to say it on her own.

Even as the day wore on, Jamie's mother never let up. She'd freshen her lipstick again and again, usually after dabbling at the meal tray and eating maybe two mouthfuls. Jamie, who'd never worn makeup, was fascinated and repelled by this routine; she would watch her mother blotting the extra by pressing her lips together, then reaching for a tissue and blotting afresh. To Jamie, it looked as though her mother were kissing her own lips, kissing paper, printing her kiss — anything but bestowing it.

When there was nothing else to do, Jamie would keep herself busy by straightening things on the bed or the sink, fussing with the flowers the volunteers kept on bringing, and with the get-well cards from faraway admirers, unknown names from unimaginable places, that never stopped coming. One had a French poodle on the front. She — it must have been a she — was decked in a ballroom dancer's skirt that billowed out from its tight waist and fitted bodice. She wore bows, too. And dancing shoes. Inside it said: "Waltz right on out of there! Get well quick!" It didn't matter what the picture was, whether of an Aladdin's lamp with a genie riding a gust of smoke that twisted from its mouth, tumbling like a leaf on a gust of wind, or a tea tray with flowers, or a teddy bear with a hot water bottle on his head, the message amounted to the same thing: "Hurry up and get better." Or: "Hope you're back on your feet soon. . . ."

"You'll feel like new when this is over. . . ." "Fly out of there! . . ." "Hope you're really better soon. . . ."

Jamie spent a great deal of time fussing in the room, handling her mother's things, but she avoided touching her mother's hands. They were cold, unnaturally cold, for one thing. That wasn't the only reason, though. How often had she touched her mother's hands when they were warm? It was so hard to untangle these thoughts. Much easier to plump her mother's pillows and smooth the sheets. She was kind to her mother's slippers, arranging them neatly, toes aligned, placing them exactly where her mother's feet would touch down at the side of the bed if she ever decided to go walking again. But, of course, that wasn't likely.

Earlier this morning, stooping to place the slippers just so, Jamie had recalled, after a space of decades, how, as a child, she'd continued to wait for her mother to come back home long after she'd been told this wasn't going to happen. She'd waited, although without hope, because it was better than not waiting. When aunts and uncles visited, she'd hide their shoes, so they couldn't get away easily. The relatives learned to make a game of it, the last morning of a visit always spent in hide-and-seek, but it hadn't been a game for Jamie.

It won't be long, Jamie said to herself, thinking of what the night nurse had told her: "Could happen any time now. Days — hours, maybe. Any unfinished business, anything you've got to say, say it while you've still got her beside you."

Say it now, right this very minute, Jamie prodded herself. Yet — what was there to say? And *who* needed to say it? She wanted to ask: Did you ever love us? Love *me?* But what was the use? What could anybody say now, so late in the day? All Jamie could do was to keep on combing.

"Got something for you!" one of the nurses, entering the

room, announced brightly. Jamie glanced at her watch. They kept advancing the time, "keeping ahead of the pain," as the doctor had promised. The medication was only for pain now — morphine in grape juice, squirted under the tongue. The nurse brought it in a syringe without a needle that looked like an eyedropper. The liquid was blue in the syringe; Jamie's mother called it blue wine, tipping her head back and opening her mouth for it without having to be urged.

This particular nurse was new to Jamie, although she seemed to know her mother. "How's the dancer doing?" she asked. At the word *dancer* — Jamie saw it — her mother twinged. "How about a whirlpool bath?" the nurse went on. Jamie's mother shook her head.

"I guess not now" — Jamie tried to soften her mother's refusal — "maybe later."

The nurse promised to come back later on to see whether she'd changed her mind, waved, and disappeared. Jamie's mother shook her head again.

"Why not?" Jamie asked after the nurse left. "You liked it before. It would relax you. After a while, maybe?"

"Not — ever," Jamie's mother said under her breath. She'd spoken so faintly, Jamie wasn't sure she'd understood at first. Then her mother cleared her throat; she spoke quite distinctly. "I'm so tired," she said. "Tired and weary . . ."

"Tired of baths?" Jamie asked.

"Tired and weary," her mother repeated. "Of everything. Tired of baths and pottying. Of mornings, noons, and nights. Of sitting up and lying down. Tired of being tired . . ."

Jamie, who'd not been expecting this, had no reply ready. "I guess you must be" was all she could think to say.

She was even less prepared for what came next. "When will it be?" her mother asked quietly. They both knew what "it" meant, no need for spelling it out, and her mother closed her eyes while she waited for the answer.

Jamie could hear her own sharp intake of breath, like a match being struck, before she spoke the word.

"Soon," she said.

I'm Still Here

TUESDAY: Louellen's second day on the job. She really doesn't want to leave the open air, the to-ing and fro-ing of traffic on the boulevard. She's not at all eager to pass through that door. Not that it's so hospitable outside; far from it: it's spring, how it always is late in March here in the Texas Panhandle: one minute, the smell of sage in wet ditches; the next, feedlot. Sudden crossing winds, like they're trying to wrap everything up into the tightest bundle, then, just as furiously, *un*wrap it.

Only a couple minutes to go. Louellen's almost there. She's scheduled for a 3:00 P.M. to midnight slot; it's a little off standard for the convenience of the staff members who are training her. Already, Louellen notices, the professional good-time girls are commencing their early shift on the boulevard, getting set for happy hour. One of them, a little gal in lemon-colored smock and tights, waves to the passing cars from her perch on the bus bench, this looping come-hither motion, like she's hauling in a fish line. She looks a little hectic, flushed — too much rouge or the wind. What makes Louellen look twice is: she's got a belly on her like she's eight months gone. Must be desperate for money but, you have to wonder, who would buy? Could be a kinky sex thing, of course. Ordinarily, Louellen would say the situation was pretty sick, yet right now, considering her new job, it looks almost like health to her. Part of Louellen doesn't ever want to leave the world where women fresh-up their lipstick and tighten the hoops in their ears.

Her breath catches — the building in sight. Louellen is surprised — dismayed — by her shakiness. The first time she entered the hospice building she could excuse it, but not today. A truly strange feeling . . . like that instant when you jump and neither foot yet touches the ground. You know how the heart lurches? Well, that instant — stretched. The outer door swings open, rocks a little, falls shut. How long can that take? *Long,* believe it. Louellen isn't over the shaky feeling yet. This isn't just *any* door, is what she's thinking. Even today, her second day, she's spooked —

— But presses forward into the vestibule. Nods to the founder's portrait, the first thing she sees. It's Sister Rosaleen: her eyes are steely blue.

Those eyes miss nothing. Louellen is reminded of all the touching up she's done to get ready for today — the peach blush for sallow cheeks, the faint smear of lilac eye shadow on each sleep-fattened lid. The blunt, blue-suited figure in the painting, with her barely combed thatch of white hair, could not be more different. A woman sure of her use. "Here's how I am," she seems to say, "take it or leave it." With pudgy fingers she grips a red rose on a long stem — it could be a clarinet or a plunger, the way she's got it — holding it out from her chest. It was Sister Rosaleen who started this hospice, then, everything set, moved on. Working someplace near Houston now. Up to something. Louellen hadn't paid that much attention when the story was told to her.

Now Louellen enters the unit. There's an odor here, quieter than anything the wind drags through the streets. She only notices it when she stands at this threshold, before it surrounds her completely. Something faint, muted, musty, tallowy . . . oversweet. It isn't a mystery, though. With little effort, she can name the elements: air freshener and lanolin, coffee endlessly brewing. Stool — the traces rubbed over, erased, but not entirely. Disinfectant. Talcum powder. Flowers. Fear and flowers . . .

Flowers and fear.

Louellen detours to the ladies' to give herself a minute more adjustment time. Runs a quick comb through her hair — why didn't she use spray on a day like this? Lipstick's still glossy: she's ready as she'll ever be. She locks up her purse, signs in.

The reason Louellen's back into working is she needs a change, something to take her mind off Ray's walking out on seventeen years of marriage, a marriage she'd flattered herself was rock solid. No kids, sad to say, but that was his problem — Ray's — he'd had a bad case of mumps as a five-year-old, so it was he who couldn't. But they were happy enough together, just the two of them. Or so she'd thought. Then he walked out. Said he was tired of it, wasn't anybody's fault.

What was it? She bowled, he roped; he liked canyons, she preferred malls. They'd always had different interests, but wasn't that how it was supposed to be? She'd get up in the mornings after Ray left and roam from room to room, finding everything the same and not the same — untouched except for his clothes being gone. The only other thing he'd taken was his van.

Louellen found herself taking small steps moving through the house, navigating each turn as if unsure what might be coming up around the bend. Familiar things were touched with strangeness: whether it was the clockface over the stove beaming black rays or the silver-framed wedding couple still standing arm and arm on the dresser, now smiling to the facing wall, the glazed air, the unvisited bed. She was struck by all the doubles: two toothbrushes in the glass, twin terry-cloth bathrobes hanging from branched hooks back of the bathroom door, the pair of matching coffee mugs she used to set out in the mornings — pairs, sets, twins, twos together everywhere her glance happened to fall.

Nothing counted: faith, feeling, promises, years. . . . It wasn't only the house that mocked her. She'd be standing there in front of the mirror, one hand tugging at the loosening skin between her neck and chin, eyebrow pencil in the other hand, wondering why she still bothered. Who for? Nothing connected: she'd get all fixed up, then stay inside, behind walls, for the rest of the day.

Louellen told herself things could have been worse but, thinking it over, she wasn't sure. Ray had never once struck her — back of his hand or words. Sometimes she thought it might have been better if he had lashed out, if he'd left her bruised and aching — but *feeling*. All he'd done at the last was to shut the door on their life together, and walk away from the house with Louellen still inside it. As if he'd only been visiting all those years, as if the marriage had never been. Louellen couldn't even cry. He'd canceled her out.

It went on like that until last week, when her car quit. She'd been driving north on the boulevard when it happened. Full stop. Not even a sputter from the ignition. The lucky part was its happening at a stoplight. Louellen switched on the hazards, forgetting to be thankful that they, at least, still worked, opened the car door, stepped out, and — just lost it. Lost it!

Didn't know what came over her. Stood there, smack to the yellow line, cars swarming past, doing their best to loop around her, the drivers gaping, honking, giving her the finger — Louellen never-minding them, too busy beating up on her car. She started in kicking the wheels, the fenders, the door, then backed up to make them good *long* kicks. She pounded the hood with her fists, slapping the metal, her palms burning, letting the four-letter words fly —

— Until this old couple, in a rusted-out jalopy even junkier than hers, slowed past her to the corner and parked there. From the side of her eye she'd caught a glimpse of them, their blurry white heads leaning in to one another, consulting, then the old man stooping, shutting the car door behind him, slanting towards her. Gently, he steered her over to the curb where the wife was waiting.

There they stood, the two of them smoothing her shoulders until Louellen let loose and wept for very shame. The gas station they drove her to was only a couple blocks off; had she lifted her head she might have known it all along. What this little incident told her loud and clear was how much she needed to get back out into the world. Needed to get out of her head — fast as she could. She had to have a job to go to, it wasn't only a question of money.

Louellen had been a licensed vocational nurse before she married and had worked, off and on, whenever their finances became stressed, so it wasn't as if she'd be entering cold. She wanted something a little different than she'd done before, though, and browsing the classifieds, happened to light on an ad for hospice work, training provided. She'd shown up for the interview, and now here she was. She thought she could handle it — it didn't sound too strenuous. She thought there might even be a kind of safety in it, knowing what to expect, no great surprises. A quiet place, after all. No code blues signaling *get here get here* over the intercom, no heroics — nothing you could do to change things. Not much you could do to mess up.

The nurse in charge — a new one from yesterday — asks her would she mind rounding up the last of the lunch trays, so Louellen goes from room to room, checking. It's a good way of seeing who the patients are and in what condition. Most of the late trays are untouched, she finds, or picked over only a little. A few crumbs of cake, a sip of juice, a spoonful of mashed potato . . .

Lunch trays are no sooner collected than Louellen's called to get a room ready for a new admission, something she already knows how to do. It's peaceful work, nobody hassling her. She opens the curtains so whoever's coming won't feel boxed in. Same wild weather: the trees still dashing their heads together in the wind. She presses her hand to the chill glass. She stares at her hand and at the bird feeder close to the window with no more interest in one than in the other. The bird feeder is stuffed with seed, but no birds are biting. Must be the wind.

Next come the supper trays. Louellen gets them round. Two she takes back immediately; the patients are beyond eating, and their visitors aren't interested either. Another patient died earlier in the day, so that's three trays unclaimed. Shame to go to waste. Louellen ate just before she left the house, so she can't. As it turns out, though, only one of the trays will go begging. A couple of nurses are interested: they hunch over the meal cart, taking their supper standing. Working twelve-hour shifts, their appetites are good. Louellen, standing in for them at the front desk, can't help listening in.

They talk about medication schedules, and a patient who's been readmitted from home care because she's been vomiting blood, about a cutting horse exhibit coming up, and Dr. Mackey's new wife, and a sale on VCRs at Sears that has only one more day to go. Then they start in on one of the patients who plucked a carnation from his bud vase and slipped the stem under his tongue, thinking he was taking his temperature. Louellen guesses it's the man in 104. He's in a dreamworld, all right. When she went in to take his tray, he was sound asleep, but his hands and feet were busy. The man was a dentist — someone in the family had propped up a plaque on the windowsill to prove it — and it looked like he was doing dentistry in his dream. He kept on making those fine little rolling motions with his fingertips that Louellen recalled from her own dentist, Dr. Bates, when he picked out a drill bit or shaped tiny balls of silver for a filling. And one foot kept pressing down and letting up, working an imaginary pedal. He was drilling in his dream, Louellen figured, still at it.

But now Fern arrives. She's the one supposed to show Louellen the ropes. Since she was off yesterday, Louellen expects to be tagging after her most of today. Fern's been at this job for years, she gathers, some kind of nurse, not registered, but trusted. When there's a quiet moment, Louellen will ask outright, or maybe try for a closer reading of her badge.

"What next?" Louellen asks. She likes to have a little warning in advance.

"Bed bath in 108," Fern says, and she instructs Louellen what to bring from the supply room.

The sign on 108 says "Betty Loomis" and, slashed beside it, her doctor's name. It's dim inside; there's a fan going. "I think she's active," Fern whispers, standing over the bed. "Active" is shorthand for actively dying. The patient does seem completely out of it. Maybe she still hears, though — they say that hearing is the last sense to fade. People tend to forget when the patient's as far gone as this one. Still, Fern and Louellen start out by being careful.

There are so many questions Louellen wants to ask but can't until they're out of the room. She wonders to herself how long the patient's been in this state. Must be a while, Louellen figures, since there aren't any family members or friends waiting around for developments.

Somebody should let them know — shouldn't they? — if she's really active.

She's breathing hard, the patient is, despite her oxygen hookup. It's noisy: phlegm bubbles up in her throat; she's no longer able to swallow. Fern suctions her mouth, and that seems to ease things for the time being. One of the patient's hands is cold, mottled, and blue; the other hand's burning up; the nails on both are curled under. She's wearing a *Do-not-resuscitate* bracelet on her left wrist, the side that's already gone. Despite the icy left arm and the fan spinning away full speed on the window ledge, her pillow is drenched with perspiration.

The television's going: a man and a woman talking about tabletop sex. It's chatter, only half serious but, coming into this room at this moment, seems to Louellen outrageous, deranged. Heartbreaking, really, though no hearts break. Louellen, for her part, raises not a peep of protest. She's too new, she tells herself, and she's seen the television running in so many of the rooms, sound on or sound off; nobody seems to notice. When her own time comes, though, Louellen wants the world to stop. Is a minute too much to ask?

Even when the television voices drop so low they're almost white noise, the images — garish, startling, too bright — leap in the darkened room, and Louellen's eyes can't help but follow. She notices that the guest expert is wearing a pink suit with no blouse, how the guest expert crosses her legs slowly, stroking her knee, how the camera strokes with her, gliding smooth as silk down her full calf, taking a little twirl at the ankle, then rising again.

And it's Fern, actually, who draws Louellen back to the task at hand. "CPD," she mouths the letters silently; Louellen has to lip-read. Not that Betty Loomis would understand what the letters mean. CPD is shorthand for cardiopulmonary disease.

When Louellen is sent to the closet for a change of clothes, the first thing she sees is empty hangers and there aren't any shoes. Just two shirts, a bed jacket, and three pairs of pastel panties nearly folded in an open suitcase on the floor, that's all — nothing else for below the waist. Like Betty's already half-disappeared. Louellen fetches a shirt. It's a pretty one, the print's of water lilies, looks like silk.

"Betty?" Fern's busy trying to make contact: "Betty! Can you hear me? Press my hand if you hear me, okay?" But if Betty hears, she's not saying. Not saying, or signing. Very little movement of any kind that Louellen can make out. Her eyes are only a crack open, same as when they first came in.

They roll her over to Louellen's side first and, while Louellen holds the torso secure, Fern goes over the patient's back gently with lukewarm water and shaving foam — the only soap mild enough to be used here. Fern's attention is plainly drifting; she fits the washcloth to the hollow of an armpit as if cleaning out a cup. But there's nothing else doing, so Louellen can't blame her for keeping an eye on the television as she works. As Louellen, too, is doing at this moment, for it's gone from talk show to news flash — a shoot-out at Willy's Burger, a cashier in a blood-spattered uniform telling how she thought the popping sounds were coming from the fryer. The cashier's voice is shrill with excitement; not a word is lost. Fern washes, Louellen dries. The patient's face, neck, and hands are old, but above the ankles and below the neck, Betty Loomis is still young, smooth, and slender. Fern powders everywhere, all the folds.

Rolling and turning her, they change the undersheet, reposition her in bed. Louellen doesn't know whether this is painful for the patient, whether she feels anything at all. She seriously questions whether the patient even knows they're here.

But then, all of a sudden, the patient's eyes spring open. They're deep, bright blue, deeply shocked. She's staring, eyes fastened on the ceiling, blinded or dazzled. "Coma vigil" — the words pop into Louellen's head. Something like that.

Pretty unnerving — whatever it's called. What does the patient see, Louellen wonders? Anything? Eyes so wide, pupils dilated like it's dark but there's some sort of light show going on right above. Louellen follows the patient's gaze, but all she can see are the gray, pocked soundproofing panels — ordinary ceiling.

"She's angel gazing," Fern announces.

The patient is still doing it — whatever it is she's doing — with her eyes, and Louellen glances up at the ceiling once more, again trying to make out what she sees. Angels? Could be, she guesses. Anything *could* be. Or she could be dreaming with her eyes open, who could say?

Then her eyes close. She's completely slumped. "Let's get her head up a little," Fern says. They grip the ends of the folded drawsheet close in, and heave. "Now turn her towards me."

The patient is lying on her other side now, facing Fern and the door, her knees drawn up. They cram an extra pillow behind her back to keep her supported, a pillow between her legs to keep her knees from rubbing. This seems to do it.

Although she really doesn't look all that much more comfortable after their efforts, there's not much else they can do.

They turn over the head pillow to give her a fresh surface — the other side's so damp. They pull up the top sheet, the cotton blanket, and reset the bed rails, then pause a minute, standing there on opposite sides of the bed, in case there's one last thing they might be forgetting. The patient's eyes are closed now, only the faintest splinter of white showing.

"That's a nice ring," Fern says all of a sudden. "Those real rubies?"

"This?" Louellen stretches her hand over the bed. "They're carnelian. Only semiprecious." It's the ring Ray gave her when they got engaged. She'd put away her wedding ring, but this one she just couldn't.

"Real pretty." Fern takes Louellen's hand and tilts it to the light. "What'd you say your name was — Lois?"

Louellen tries to tell her again, but the word is lost in a burst of television laughter. They're talking across the patient, she realizes.

"Please? You say Louise?" Fern asks.

"Louellen," she says it louder this time, and even starts in spelling it: "L-O-U-" But now somebody else is chiming in —

It's Betty Loomis from her bed. Her eyes are open. "Elh . . . oh . . . *ohhh* . . . ehm . . ." Each letter breathed out with care, as if it mattered, even now. Loud and slow, the full name comes. *Her* name: Loomis. Then, as if nothing had ever happened, as if Louellen's out of her head or dreaming the whole thing up, Betty's back to where she was, eyes shut, her breath just frothing the air. But she's here, Louellen marvels, that's what she's telling them. Even now. Straddling two worlds maybe, but still here.

Greyhound

ONE OF THE WOMEN, a social worker, he *thinks* — he's never clear who does what in this place — asks Paul if he has any unfinished business. What a question! "You mean — besides the whole rest of my life?" he comes back at her. "Anything special on your mind?" She doesn't let up. The answer is obvious: Amber. But Paul will not let the name pass his lips.

"Want to talk about it?"

Paul shakes his head, then turns his face away and pretends to sleep until he does sleep and the woman goes.

When Paul gets back to the house — in what shoes? — he has no shoes on his feet. This bothers him, because how could he? He's been walking or running for ages. Has no idea where he's been. "My shoes got tired," he says aloud, lips moving on their own, "had to leave 'em behind."

He recalls rain, high winds, money blowing loose. Green bills scooting by, nobody chasing after them. Could be leaves blowing for all anybody seems to care. But somebody does care — a bunch of fists slam into his chest — Paul's folding, got to, bowing into the muddy street . . .

He wakes in pain, the dream still bruising, real as anything.

Paul isn't often in pain these days, mostly just strange to himself and, so the nurse tells him, "dozing on and off, confused." She's only partly right: sleeping and waking blend into one another, sure, but he's not confused by it. That's how things go. What's weird is feeling jittery and slack, both at the same minute. But, really, he has never seen so clear. He can't outrun this: he has no shoes — no legs to speak of. His feet are swollen, his legs might be covered in bark; they're clods now, heavy, numb — rooted. Oxygen lightly fizzing his nostrils, he surveys the sheet that covers him, the mound of rib cage, the ledge of toes, his mind alighting and moving on without dwelling anyplace. He replays his memories, whatever comes up. Waking and dozing aren't that different anymore. Never were. He can hear children's voices, running footsteps, in the hallway — he doesn't think he's dreaming this, but can't be absolutely sure he isn't. These days, he dreams with the light streaming in, the window curtains, the curtains of his eyes, wide apart. Now that he's about to leave it, life looks to him like a dream, among many dreams — a very bright one.

He takes a lot of walks in his mind. What he misses most, stalled on this narrow slab of a bed, is being able to leave at will, his old habit of putting distance between himself and whatever is boxing him in at the moment. The incredible ease of it: shutting the door behind him, stepping clear of walls, into a wash of air and motion. Stepping out of his old life, free and clear. He could do it any minute. Never needed much — only a roof and three squares a day. Two squares, really, if it came to that; he knew how to get by.

He'd stayed put for only months at a time. Been a bike messenger, a movie cashier; worked sales: hardware, carpets, other stuff. Even had a desk job once in auto supplies — had a chair on a swivel, in basket, out basket, the works; he lasted all of three weeks at that.

What he misses, too, are the long treks he took by bus clear across the country, East Coast to West and back, seeking work, escape from work, keeping tabs on girlfriends, hooking up and splitting whenever things got heavy. Moving with the flow, town and countryside dissolving, flowing past, never real enough to hold him for long.

Only one sticking point: the last time.

If he concentrates now maybe he can make things turn out different. He's working on that last trek, the one with all the rain, the joker . . . what's-'is-face . . . from Yonkers. And the heart surgery lady, hogging the double seat. But that was later. So long a before and after, so little time between with the girl, Amber. . . . If only he could revise the part with Amber in it by a week, a day even, be granted just a little more time. But all he'll ever have is that one night.

The trip was back in February, a whole lifetime away, and yet, hard to believe, barely two months back. Times and seasons blur, but not this one. Only a feeling of fullness in his side, didn't amount to anything at first, then the tightness he'd put down to stress. No idea what was coming, simply another getaway, he thought, shaping up like so many others.

. . . And starting off where all his trips started — at the Port Authority Terminal in Manhattan, no lockers to be had, none provided — for fear of bombs. Which means sitting on your duffel for hours. Viewing the passing scene at knee level, Paul follows the antics of panhandlers dancing loops round the security patrol. It's amusing for the first five minutes. Ten at most. A hooker in running shoes comes up to him, a bottle blonde who's tired of trying; her yellow hair has long black roots. She says something to him he can't make out — sounds like "tonka t'ya" — then, abruptly, backs off. A maintenance man edges towards him with a mop; Paul doesn't budge; the mop doesn't insist. His duffel forms an island with Paul king of his small hill.

Despite everything, Paul's feeling hopeful; he always feels hopeful when setting out. Only this lineup is a drag. Too much time on his hands, and he ends up brooding on what he's running away from. He's out of work at the moment, though that's not why he's on the move. This time, it's the girlfriend. Been shacked up with Judy going on half a year. That long? Ought to have his head examined. It's saved on rent, of course, but, in every other respect, it's cost him — *plenty*. She expected him to account for everything — time, money, the pals he hung out with. Kept trying to pry into his mind, laying traps for him, wanting to know his "plans," their "prospects." He had no plans; *prospects* wasn't a word in his vocabulary. The nicer the place looked, the tighter the screws. Felt like a brace, an iron hoop, slowly closing round his ribs. Only thing he *could* do was split — stacking the miles in between himself and her. He's headed for L.A. because he has a pal there, and because it's clear across — far as he can get. What he intends to do isn't as shapely as a plan — more like a reflex. More like gasping for air. Anybody feeling what he feels would do the same.

Meantime, the minutes drag on. The waiting will end, he knows, and he will leave, set out, arrive to leave again. This direction, that direction — it looks like freedom, but it's really just a bigger swivel chair. Paul sees this, but so what? Seeing and knowing don't change a thing. He waits eagerly for the boarding gate to open, as if for the first time.

The conductor takes his own sweet time checking and double-checking their tickets and seating arrangements. The man who lands beside Paul is handicapped in some way yet to be revealed. Paul doesn't like crips and, as a firm rule, avoids them. The cheerful kind, as this one turns out to be, is especially hard to stomach. This one has a folding metal cane he stows under the seat along with a paper shopping bag. He wears a billed cap that might be glued to his head. Hours to go and he never takes it off. The hat has TOP GUN embroidered in orange on the crest.

"First time I've been on a hound in years," he says, wrestling the chair back to a more comfortable slant. He's going as far as Pittsburgh — too far for Paul's liking, but the bus is packed, there's no room for rearrangement.

"Do you like humor?" he asks.

Paul shrugs: what kind of question is that?

Straightway the man bends over and rummages in his shopping bag. Comes up with what looks like a photo album, but there are no photos in it. It's full of loose-leaf paper instead, the pages covered with block-letter printing. The man sticks out his hand before starting in on the loose-leaf. "Sam Wofford," he says, "from Yonkers. And you're — ?" What can he do? Paul is obliged to offer his name in return. He only gives his first, though. Sam doesn't seem to notice; he's into the book now, using it more as a prompter, reciting more than reading: "Can you tell me how long girls should be kissed?" The answer is: "Same as short ones." Another: "Where is kindness always found?" Answer: "In the dictionary." When Sam seems to catch on to the fact that Paul isn't even smiling, he skips ahead to another section in the album. He licks his finger to pick out a special page. "How's this?" — he glances up eagerly — "I've got a whole bunch of radish jokes here. Got it — '*bunch*'?" Paul hunkers down in his seat; he's in for it. "Ever hear the joke about the guy who's got radishes in his ears?" No answer required. "Neither did he!" is the punch line. How long will this keep up? There's nothing to see once the tunnel's behind them. The Jersey flats stretch before and alongside them, a desolation of smoke and mud. Everything's gray, even the mud bleached of color. The air thickens, inside and out. Somebody in the back of the bus starts coughing and will not stop.

Knock-knocks follow, jokes about elephants, about dentists. Sam goes on and on, like a bullhorn tipped to Paul's ear, a gag a mile. "Rain falls, but does it ever get up?" Paul forgets the answer soon as he hears it.

Up the road a ways, somewhere after Philadelphia, Sam sticks out his hand for another shake before getting off. "Laughing sure does make the time pass," he says.

There's a short layover in Pittsburgh. The next bus is a new one, state-of-the-art everything — seats, lights, overhead racks, everything shiny, smelling of unaired plastic. They're as crowded as before though. Paul has been hoping to get a seat to himself, to be able to stretch out his legs for a while, but it's not to be.

His next seatmate is a redheaded girl. Her mom sits across the aisle, just plunks the girl down beside him and shuts her eyes. Of all the dumb luck! The brat starts right off — an interrogation. "Do you like being you?" she asks. Paul frowns and shrugs. "Do you like your nose?" she asks. Sore point — how does she know? Paul makes a face.

"I like your nose," she says, touching the bump from a long ago biking accident. "I like it." Paul has nothing to say to this.

"My tooth is rockety," she says. "See" — and pushes a front tooth, making it waggle, with her tongue. "I'm getting big."

"Bet you are," Paul says. "Bigger every day."

"Almost bigger," says the girl.

When Paul turns away to look out the window, she starts in kicking. "Quit it!" Paul snaps back. He's had it now.

But the girl says she didn't do it. "My shoe moved," she says.

"Your foot is in your shoe! Your foot moves your shoe. Your head moves your foot." Paul raises his voice, hoping the girl's mother will catch it — but no, she's still sleeping or faking it.

"You're funny." The girl smiles. In her own small way, she's flirting, Paul realizes. "In school we clap five times without saying anything," she says. "Then we put our heads down."

"Do that now," Paul says. They're in West Virginia, and the hills are giving him a seasick feeling.

Mercifully, mother and daughter go off at Steubenville, and not a minute too soon. In their place comes an old man who dozes his two stops. Never says a word, for which Paul is truly grateful. But the respite is brief.

The sleeper is followed by a gray-headed lady, a widow, who waits maybe five minutes before confiding all her business to Paul. Amazing what people will say to a stranger. . . . She's been helping her daughter out with a new baby. Been up all hours, sleeping on the couch. The baby gets only sugar and water in a bottle at night. The older kid is jealous and teething, has three teeth on the bottom, four on the top, as if Paul could care less. She's exhausted now and going home. . . . Where are they? Their route is turning out to be a milk run, stopping at every lost little town, some of them so small that the driver has to unlock the bus depot and load and unload the freight box himself. He calls it the lock box and makes a joke of threatening to lock up any passengers who get rowdy or take "silly powder" or smoke "left-handed cigarettes." The driver's not against smoking — he happens to be a smoker himself — and, while smoking onboard is prohibited by federal regulation, he's fitted in breaks for it, two so far.

Soon the widow is talking with another lady in the seat ahead of her, same wheel of words going round, an unbroken yattattatt, it's driving Paul crazy. Even when one of them can't hear the other over the drone of the bus, that doesn't slow them down a bit. "Is what?" the widow says. "Is what what?" says the other.

Time to take a leak. Excusing himself, Paul makes his way to the back of the bus. It's dark there, a couple of couples necking and petting — but quietly, not the usual partying free-for-all. Nobody says boo as he passes down the aisle. He notices a girl curled up on two seats, her arms folded over her face. She's barefooted — her feet must be cold. Strange . . . Paul can't recall seeing her get on, but he forgets her as he tends to his business, only glancing her way again as he steps out the door, latrine light spilling over her hair. There's a name for hair like that — not blonde, not gold, but whiter, finer. It comes to him: ash . . . ash blonde, he's never had a picture for it before. He claps the door behind him: hair and girl return to shadow. Paul takes a few steps down the aisle, but pauses when he comes to her, certain that she's awake. She's crying, trying to hide it, he's sure of it. He doesn't know what tells him this, for there are no outward signs — no heaving shoulders, no harsh breathing — she's as motionless as a living, breathing person can be. Nor does he know what possesses him when suddenly he reaches up and presses the overhead light switches. "Hey!" She squirms, shielding her eyes with both hands. "What's the big idea?"

"Too early for bed," Paul says, surprising himself with how decisive he sounds. "What's it to you?" she asks. She looks about fourteen, fifteen. "I don't know yet," Paul says. "Mind if I sit down?" She could refuse — she doesn't have to consent, but, surprisingly, without a word, she sits up, sliding over to the window seat, making room for him. She avoids looking him in the face, though.

"If you sleep now, you won't be able to later," he says, and then, by way of an opener, asks, "Do you like humor?"

"What a dumb question," she says. He'd thought so, too. "It helps make time pass," he says. And the jokes do come in handy. He launches right into one of the radish jokes.

She doesn't laugh, but she doesn't tell him to quit, either. She stares out the window, whether at their reflections in the glass or at the nothing passing by, Paul can't tell.

Right now Paul wishes he'd listened better; he's quickly nearing the end of all he recalls of Sam's long recital. He asks: "Where is kindness always found?"

And that seems to do it. Even before the punch line, she's opened up; the tears can't be held in. She swipes at the wetness with the heel of her hand, making a smear of tears and snot. When Paul asks her name, she tells him it's Amber. Then he says, and it's true, that he's never known anybody before her with a name such as that.

She isn't, by the longest stretch, beautiful — not any of the three or four types that have ever appealed to Paul. Paul himself has never been a terrific looker — what he's had is height, and energy some called nerve, a bit of daring. Amber has no energy, she's pale and thin — "skinny," he'd have to say — with narrow chest and hips. It occurs to him that she might be a year or two younger than his first guess, a kid, really. Just a runaway kid. Paul — hard to believe he's pushing thirty — is old enough to know better. He doesn't know what's gotten into him, he wants nothing more than to sit at her side all night long, breathing in her faint gingery scent, smoothing her fine-spun hair, folding her hand in his. He needs to find out how their fingers fit together: it's important. He wants to warm her bare feet between his palms. It's all so corny, Paul can hardly believe it's himself wanting this.

"Aren't your feet cold?" he asks.

"I don't care," she says, "it makes no difference to me."

Her story comes together by bits and pieces after they've made a stop in Fairview and another in Middlebourne. Both are unscheduled; everybody is ordered to remain seated inside the bus while the driver hops out. As the driver's explaining this, she's already into her shoes, and, the minute he hops outside, she's bolting. Paul — fearing he'll lose her — follows. Each time, she makes it to the phone, dials a long-distance number (collect), and gets no answer. Returning to the bus after her second try, she makes no effort to hide her tears. And then Paul learns that she's eloping, or believes she is, traveling all the way form Mingo Junction in West Virginia to Dallas, to join up with this boy — Buck — she met and dated after a concert in Wheeling. He'd promised to come back and marry her, but never did come back, so she's going to him. Paul hasn't the heart to ask how long ago this happened. There's been no answer at the number he gave her. Still — she's going to him. She trusts him.

She'd been going crazy, living with her granny, her mom's mom, when she met Buck. She and her granny couldn't pass the time of day without screaming at each other. Her mom had married again and had three other kids, one right on top of the other, kids that she — Amber — had no wish to baby-sit for. There'd been nobody else but Granny for her to go to. She didn't know whether her dad was living or dead; she'd only seen him in a photo. It was impossible for her to think of him as a dad; he was a teenager with an Elvis haircut in the picture.

Zanesville to Etna . . . somewhere along this route, they become established seatmates. They share a supper of chips, doughnuts, and Coke. Share a lot of crumbs. In Columbus, Ohio, next to the bank of video games, there's something

called a rotary merchandiser, a sort of wish-want machine —
this spinning tray full of doodads in see-through plastic boxes.
In the midst of all the humming, clacking, shrilling, zapping,
and whomping of the video games, it spins silently. For a dol-
lar in quarters you can take a swipe with the mechanical arm
at whatever box you choose. Paul and Amber stand side by
side — she comes to just under Paul's shoulder — peering into
the boxes as they go by. There's a miniature Barbie, a pair of
crucifix earrings, a digital watch, a brass whistle, a rattlesnake
breaking out of an egg, a charm bracelet. . . . Paul wants to
aim for the charm bracelet, but Amber pulls him away, saying
she'd rather have another bag of chips.

Without any words of saying so, Paul knows they'll be together all the way to St. Louis. Knows too that they'll both
have to change in St. Louis and go their separate ways. But
there's a long road ahead yet, and Paul isn't going to think
about it until he has to. Only: now, now, now. Now he's circling her wrist between his thumb and forefinger. Now they're
comparing the size of their hands, placing them side by side,
then one on top of the other — how clumsy Paul's seem, like
wooden scoops — with hers so fine boned and swallowed up
in his. Now they are linking fingers. Now he pretends to bite
the ends of her hair, but they both know he's only tickling his
lips. She starts laughing, can't help herself; then, recalling that
she'd been crying just a few minutes before, bursts into tears
again. It's a roller coaster. After the tears, she thinks maybe she
has a fever. Paul lightly presses the back of his hand to her forehead, then to his own. It's hard to tell: she's warmer than he is,
but not hot. Paul feels he's coming closer and closer, gaining
her trust. Strangely, it matters: her faith in him.

Outside of Dayton, she busies herself with her hair, making
a tail of it, twisting it through a cloth holder, looks like a

rosette, a "scrunchy" or "bunchy" some such, Paul forgets whatever it is she calls it. What he can't forget is her long white neck coming clear, or his wanting to sculpt it with his tongue. When the bus stops next she jumps to her feet, but Paul grabs her by the belt, and it's well he does, for the stop lasts scarcely a minute. They make a game of it after that. Like an infant in one of those harnesses, she pops up ready to run, whenever the bus turns into a town, and Paul grabs her to him. An hour later, they halt by the side of the road, no town or lights in sight. Amber, who's standing, notices that the driver is doing something funny, fooling around with the windshield wipers. What makes it weird is that it isn't raining. Paul stands too, to see better. Sure enough: the driver is fiddling with the wipers, testing them manually. At the next stop, he hails a mechanic who detaches a wrench from his belt and sets to tightening the middle joints. Before they set off again, the driver gives the wipers a test run. They're of some newfangled design, triple-jointed. The right one seems out of phase with the left, but Paul wonders whether maybe it's designed that way to keep the driver from falling asleep. He turns to Amber, in that cramped space, pulling her to him, the length of her against the length of him, and their lips brush. He can taste the salt. The bus moves into thickening dusk, the passengers fret or doze restlessly, no rain falls.

And then it comes — in buckets, the rain darkening the already dark, the road ahead barely a glimmer. Amber's stretched out with her calves over Paul's thighs; Paul is massaging her feet in his hands. She must be used to going barefoot — the skin of her soles is so rough. He's begun to trace the chain of her ankle bracelet, getting up nerve to ask who put it there. Back in Paul's high school days, they called them slave bracelets. Do they now? he wonders. He can barely hear himself think over the loudness of the rain. It's a blinding, clattering rain, the windshield wipers adding their cluppety-clack to the din, by now the left one crazily out of sync with the right. It's impossible to talk. The driver is slowing to a crawl when — Paul can't believe his eyes — the wipers fly off, left, right. He knows it can't be so, they must have dropped off, but flown off is what he saw. The driver curses. The bus grinds to a halt. Paul draws Amber still closer to him.

When they start to move again, completely blinded, it's at a snail's pace and only a short way up the road, where lights are blazing. Turns out to be some giant hotel-motel deal. The driver orders them not to move while he goes in to negotiate; he leaves the motor running, the overhead lights on. None of the passengers is eager to follow him out into the wet. The place seems to be called The Ankle, but, no, that can't be. The letters are melting, bleeding, one into the other. Somebody in the front of the bus says he recognizes the place: it's The Antlers. That makes more sense. "The Antlers — Absolutely Modern" — when Paul works at it, he finds he can piece it out. Judging from all the lights wasting away, it's either pretty high class or pretty desperate.

When the driver returns it's to give them the high sign: they're to come on inside to wait for a mechanic or a replacement bus. He'll drive up under the awning so no one gets drenched.

Filing into the lobby, Paul is torn between fear and rejoicing at the delay. Amber makes a beeline, as he knew she would, for the bank of phones against the far wall. Paul stands behind her, hovering, as she dials. When his hand seeks her belt, she shoos it off.

He needn't have worried: it's the same business all over again: no answer, followed by tears; Amber crumples against him. Down the corridor, seeking darkness, they go. The Antlers' dining room is unlighted, set up for morning. Nobody around. It's fancy: white tablecloths, with cloth napkins folded in peaks like wigwams, and water glasses shaped like wineglasses, turned upside down. Most of the room is taken up with open tables, but they find a booth in the back and settle in close, both on the same side. Paul is hoping for time now, praying for a long delay. Never felt anything like this before. Not for anyone. He — Paul, who cannot save himself — wants — how desperately he wants! — to save the girl from herself.

She leans against him, and he pulls her closer. He wants her to tell him everything but knows he has to wait, all in her own good time, and so he does wait, with a patience he never guessed he had in him. Her head is resting on his shoulder, her tears dampen his neck.

Then, incredibly, she sleeps, her head growing painfully heavy against his chest. Paul does his best not to shift abruptly as he lifts one stiff leg, then the other onto the facing seat. He studies the white-clothed tables set up for morning and wishes for morning never to come.

She sleeps on for hours, right up to the time they board the replacement bus. Paul is terribly stiff by now; his shoulder aches, his back aches, his butt is numb. The rain has ended. It's almost light. He knows in his bones that after they separate in St. Louis, they'll never meet again. Morning comes, a busy, fussing brightness.

It's all downhill after that, with the fewest, quickest stops, the new driver bent on making time. It's all mileage. In St. Louis, Paul puts a ten-dollar bill into Amber's hand, that and a scrap of paper with the address and phone number of where he guesses he'll be staying first in L.A., wishing now for one fixed place where he could be sure to be reached.

And then they board their buses — she first, dry eyed and confident. She's got with her only a knapsack and a small metal suitcase — the kind ice-skaters carry. They kiss nervously, twice, but Paul can recall no particular sensation, no particular taste or texture to their parting kiss. He watches her bus back out, then shuts his eyes until he's sure it's completely vanished, so as not to see it diminish, becoming one more speck on the road.

Paul's bus, an hour later, is another crowded one. He's slightly nauseous now and hopes to sit up front, but the only seat to spare in the front of the bus is occupied by a woman with her legs stretched out. Paul asks if she minds his sitting beside her. She shakes her head — "sorry." Explains that she wouldn't mind at all but she's had recent heart surgery and has to keep her feet elevated. So he ends up sitting next to the person everybody else is avoiding, the man is so wasted. There's a stench about him, too. He looks old, in his sixties, maybe more, though he might be in his forties — just wasted. Turns out, he's carrying his goods in a trash bag under his seat. "Going to a brand-new city," he says. Paul doesn't bother to ask which one, pretty sure he'll be getting off when the conductor puts him off, which happens at the next stop. The man's been drinking, on top of everything — completely sloshed, though he wants it understood that he never touches the grape — "not even raisins."

Leaving St. Louis, Paul stares at the arch he'd paid no attention to coming in: exactly one-half of a McDonald's sign. Day into night — one long swirl of regret. . . . His eyes are tired, playing tricks. And there must be something coating the windows, he doesn't know whether it's sweat, grease, grime, or what: everything looks queer through the glass, smudged; the passing headlights of the cars are plumed, the streetlamps bearded. He overhears the heart surgery woman telling the driver: "You've got two choices, and they're both the same." Then: "He said his name was Frank, and maybe it was. . . . " Words blow in and out of their mouths, senseless. Behind him, a man is explaining to all who will listen how he's lost his job in the gray land and is setting out for California, where he can work out in the sun. The gold land . . . that old dream. "Can't stand people living all gobbed up together," he says. Paul's nausea is gaining. At the next rest stop, he grabs a hamburger, the first sensible food he's had in hours. It stays down, that's all he can say for it. Even drowned in ketchup, the taste is mushy metal. His nausea returns. He tries once more to sleep, manages a few hours, dreaming off and on. Right before waking, he has a long dream he mostly forgets, recalling only a skim off it. Something about standing alongside a steaming bus, standing out in the cold, trying to bum a cigarette from an old lady who's wearing a red rose stuck between her kerchief and her hair. She gives him one, a butt, half smoked down, from his own pocket — turns out she's wearing *his* jacket — so he pats the pockets for his lighter, but, when he looks at her again, she's his mother. She's trying to feed him something on the end of a fork. He turns away because he doesn't recognize it as food.

It's not a bad dream, not stressed or anything. In fact, he saw a gray-headed woman with a paper rose stuck between her kerchief and her hair in one of the stations in Missouri after Amber left. Paul has no idea what his mother might look like by now if she had lived. She'd died before he was two. All he has are a few photographs from her wedding, and a couple more taken with her a few months after he was born, but no living recollection.

Awake, he makes a fresh effort to take an interest in the

passing sights, but nothing much stands out. Seems like his whole life is here, in this moving capsule, in the middle of nowhere, suspended. Houses and sand hills, cars and cattle, blur in passage. They are nothings: shapes poured out. Somewhere in that vast emptiness west of Albuquerque, a pain seizes him — a sudden spasm knotting him from side to back — a matter of minutes only, but leaving him tight-lipped with shock and pain. It is the first hint of things to come.

When he gets to L.A., finally, the pain starts up again — bad. The doctor thinks it's gallstones, but soon as he operates, learns the real story, the cancer everywhere. Nothing to do but close him back up. Paul turns round and heads for his aunt Ada's in Wayside, back the way he's come, half-hoping that Amber would be turning that way, too, heading home, or that she would know at least how tenderly he'd held her all night through, loving for no reason, loving without taking, that such things are possible and do happen, however rarely, they do.

Air

ESPITE everything, it's close in the room. Cliff has cracked the door to the courtyard back as far as it will go, his mother has opened the door to the hallway wide, and Ellen has set the fan on high in the airway they've created between them. A few minutes ago, when a sudden gust sent the courtyard door shut — not even shut, only swinging — the old man yelled out. The way he hollered, you'd have thought they were starting to clamp the lid on him.

It's a wonder to Cliff that his father finds breath enough to protest. "Gimme a cupful of that air . . . I'll be awright," the old man whines. Over and over, the same haggling: "Little slug — just a swallow of that air. . . ." Yet, only an hour ago, when they took him at his word and wheeled his bed out into the courtyard, he felt no better. "If only I could rustle around in it . . . ," he whispered. In a way, it was worse being outside because the old man knew that if being out in that big sky he'd been so hankering for didn't ease him, then nothing would. He was fighting for every breath now — how'd he put it? — "like a honking fish." That's exactly what it looked like, too, his thrashing around on dry land, drowning in air, his mouth — the first thing you'd notice about him — wide agape.

And now the nurses have come and stand there beside his father's bed. They're a bit agitated, abuzz — something about a "DNR form" he failed to sign on admission yesterday.

There was no budging the old man then, and by now, Cliff judges, it's probably too late. Not that his father didn't know what was in store for him. First thing he said when they settled in was: "This it? The last room? Am I suppose to die in this bed — facing that damn door?" The rest of the family hemmed and hawed about nobody knowing the day or the hour, whatever people say at such times. He'd made out the Medicaid forms without a hitch, but he'd lingered over the living will. Maybe because the admission team seemed too eager. The nurse stood there, with two student nurses ready to witness his signature, right behind her. One of the prospective witnesses had even taken out her pen — that's how ready she was for a routine signing. She'd misfigured badly, though.

Cliff's father hadn't missed a thing. "Aren't you being a little previous?" He directed his gaze at the woman with the open pen. And then he refused — not flat-out refused, merely postponed, but it came to the same thing. "Let's leave things as they are for now," he said. No help for it but to back off for the time being.

The problem is: they can't leave it indefinitely, as one of the nurses explained to Cliff when the family came in. If they want heroics, they've got to get him to the hospital — right quick. They don't do resuscitations here.

"Don't work so hard, Mr. Ansley," the senior nurse says. "You don't have to push yourself." She's taking vital signs: blood pressure, pulse. They can't be good, because suddenly she steps out, the student nurses in tow. Cliff can hear them conferring in the hallway, right outside the door; he can make out words and fragments of words: what sounds like "oronaze," "Christmas tree," "cannula." He imagines that "Christmas tree" is code for something she'd rather not say openly — something like "Mayday." He more than suspects that the time of choice is past now. Anyway, they all know what the old man's wishes were before he came in; he'd been firm: no heroics.

A few minutes later the senior nurse comes round again. She's carrying the oxygen hookups: a mask, which she sets down on the sink, and something lighter, a device with branching tubes. And the "Christmas tree" — Cliff can see now why it's called that. It's a small, conical wall attachment, green, with ridges, and looks very much like a miniature pine tree. No big secret here: it hitches up to the gauge for metering the flow of oxygen. She stretches out the tubing, looping it over his father's ears, adjusting it so that the prongs enter the nostrils comfortably, then she tightens the noose under his chin. Surprisingly, the old man, with his lifelong scorn of canes and crutches, makes no protest at being tethered; he even seems to sigh with relief when she sets the device going. That done, she promises to bring something to help soothe him if he gets too agitated — "just enough to take the edge off, not enough to zonk him out" — this last remark directed over her shoulder to the other family members, but surely audible to Cliff's father.

Soon as she's out the door, Cliff, ever curious, picks up the mask to examine it more closely. It's transparent, with elastic straps for holding the thing snugly to the face. Looks something like a snorkeler's mask, only much lighter — with vents that would make it useless if it were for diving. Cliff doesn't think the nurse has simply forgotten the mask. She's left it here for later; for her, he reflects, there must be a known progression.

"What's that you were saying, Dad?" Cliff stoops over the bed.

"Thought *you* said," the old man murmurs.

Speak to him now — while you're both able, Cliff tells himself. This is the moment for it, yet he can only summon up the obvious. "I'm here, Dad" — taking his father's hand in his and pressing it. The hand is dry, as burled and twisted as old wood, the nail beds bulged, thick and blue.

There'd been time enough for a summing up yesterday, after he'd settled into hospice and had been made comfortable as could be. "It's gone fast," his father said. "Wasn't always an easy ride. If I could just get astride of this last. It's a big, large thing!" Then, when no one jumped in to assure him that he'd lick this last thing as he'd licked everything else, he'd voiced an acceptance of sorts. "Don't know what I'd do different if I could." Nothing he hadn't said half a million times already. "Been pretty damn lucky, all in all . . ."

Cliff never could fathom what his father meant by "luck." It had been a hardscrabble life down the years — and the old man was still scrabbling at the end for every particle of air, every inch of tread. He'd been an outdoorsman all his life: a wheat farmer to start, then, when that didn't pay off, sold the land and gone roving round the area doing custom cutting for his neighbors' crops, windmill repair, and whatever handiwork presented itself — cadging for odd jobs between the harvests. He'd managed to stay free of enclosures — the factory and office fates of other failed farmers, but that was the extent of his good fortune, as Cliff reckoned it. He'd held the dubious privilege of continuing to labor in the open air, battling dry earth and wind all his days.

Cliff hated the dryness, the emptiness, the harsh land that gave no shelter. Whenever he thought of the high plains, and wanted to sum up his bitterness about it in a single image, he thought of the stakes the first settlers had contrived for tethering their horses in the absence of trees. They still kept a couple of those old stakes, pampered like holy relics, in the canyon museum. They looked like instruments of torture — giant corkscrews with loops on top to which the reins were knotted. The things were twisted, screwed down into the earth deep as they would go. Only way you could count on the land in West Texas was — literally — to screw it.

Cliff hated the grinding of the wind on the plains, whether the red, gritty wind coming out of the west, or the black alluvial wind from the north, or the caliche wind, yellow and white, from the land close by. What he hated most was the ceaselessness of the wind, like a vast, malevolent spirit, brooding and breathing over the land. And taking its toll — his father now crying for air.

It was the wind that decided Cliff, early on, that he had to cut free soon as he could. He'd made that decision years before he was able to leave. He was eight at the time, playing outside with a pet pup named Rags he would never see again, and the only thing that struck him as strange was the sudden stillness. His father was getting ready to paint the window trim on the east side of the house; it was an indigo blue that Cliff had helped him to mix. Then the birds started up, and the cattle — they'd sensed something brewing long before any human had picked up on it — and Rags started whimpering. For a long moment, there wasn't any wind.

And then there was — a tidal wave. Cliff had only enough time to hurl himself under the front steps. There was a bursting pressure in his ears, the sound of windows popping. From between the slats of the fingers he held over his face, Cliff could see the roof of the house parachute up, up and up, and pieces of the shed go whirling after it. And — it would have been comical if he'd seen it in a film — there was a wet paintbrush dancing in the air.

When he ventured out of hiding, the first thing he noticed was the wide blue gash left by the paintbrush all across the un-damaged front wall, the only standing wall of the house. And that was it for Cliff — a clear sign from on high, if he ever needed one — not to count on anything lasting, in this part of the inhabited world. It took — what? less than a minute? — to rip up decades of backbreaking toil, of building, cultivating, and tending.

After the rebuilding, there'd been two good years. His father trudged ahead, ever hopeful. He had plans for Cliff — they'd work together on the land. Cliff went along, not saying, but, in his own mind, never wavering, not once reconsidering. Even when his first job in the city fell through and his father offered him security of a sort, he held firm to his resolve never to come back. He knew that his father clung with equal stubbornness to his own hope that Cliff would see the light, returning in his own good time to work beside him in his declining years and to continue after him in the days he would not live to see. It was the same stubbornness with which his father had held on all his life. Even when most of his fields were sold, he still planned on buying land again, building up "the homeplace," acre by acre. No matter how hard things got, he refused to sell his machin-ery, though his combine fell steadily in the listings from state-of-the-art in the sixties to collectible — almost antique — as time wore on.

As an only son in a family of three girls, Cliff had felt his fa-ther breathing down his neck from as far back as he could remember. His sisters were spared. Even now — aside from his mother, only Ellen is waiting with him — Leota and Kathy have so many things to do for *their* children, things that can't be put on hold. They've got their own families — they're not forever bound to the family of their childhood. Their mother, it goes without saying, will be his — Cliff's — responsibility for the rest of her life. No telling how long she'll be able to manage on her own. And then what? Maybe that's why Cliff feels so crowded in this room, as straitened, in his own way, as his father is. It's the pressure building. Even with both doors open and the curtains drawn back, he can't help feeling squeezed.

There's fight in the old man yet, though. When the lunch tray comes, he wants to rise on his own power to meet it. Cliff persuades him not to waste energy, and the old man consents to allowing Cliff to crank up the bed for him and even to have his back bolstered with an extra pillow. He's determined to eat. "Gotta keep up my strength . . . ," he says, his voice scarcely above a whisper. How pointless can you get? Cliff's mother's hands, never steady at the best of times, zigzag as she prepares to download a forkful of mashed potatoes and gravy. Trying to move the mess around in his mouth, Cliff's father ends up nearly choking on it. Cliff tries to get a sip of water to him, but he waves it away. All he really wants is air. He barely spouts the words: "Taster's gone!" pushing against the table — a futile slap that throws him limply forward. Cliff catches him under the arms. A noisy gulping of air and he lets out with, "This blooming cancer!" Another swallow of air: "It bites, it eats. . . ." Then a long, snorting breath, his chin thrust out: "It's wrote my picture in the dirt —" Same words he'd use to speak of a horse who'd thrown him.

Holding the old man upright, Cliff notices how deeply the back of his father's neck is scored; he has the sun-creased neck of a stoop laborer. Everything — face, hands, back — is tracked with his toil. Cliff scoots the table over the old man's knees, down to the foot end, then lowers the head of the bed. His father takes a long pull of oxygen, and coughs out, "More! . . . Mash . . . that button —" Cliff presses the call button for the nurse to come decide how much more; he knows he's not supposed to tamper with the oxygen on his own.

She comes, takes a quick glance at Cliff's father, and moves the dial up a notch. "That should do it for a little while," she says. "And — these should help." She's brought an attachment, which looks like a piece of dental equipment, for suctioning his mouth. Also, something she calls a scope patch. "Run that by me again, please," Cliff asks. "That Band-Aid thing you've got in your hand — what did you call it?"

"Scopalamine," she explains. It reduces the secretions of the mouth. "Absorbs like a nicotine patch — you've seen those?" She talking to Cliff, but the old man nods, as if by way of answer. Actually, he's starting to blink off. He's soon drowsing, or the equivalent, eye whites gleaming, his lids open only a sliver. He makes no response at all when the nurse applies the patch under his ear.

Cliff sits on, crossing his right knee over his left, then reversing — left over right, then reversing again — back as before. He feels nothing in particular, except when his gaze happens to fall on the windowsill, where his father's gray Stetson sits forlorn. That moldy old thing! It's as intimate a part of his father as an arm or a leg. Simply wretched — the crown nearly bashed in, the whole thing's blood spattered from decades of dehornings and the day-to-day soiling of fingers raising it, adjusting the brim.

Wouldn't you know it — his foot's asleep! Cliff needs a

walk, a little action here. His mother seems to be dozing now, so Cliff signals to Ellen, makes a pantomime of his fingers stepping (like the ad for the yellow pages), jabs at his chest to indicate *he'll* be doing the walking — not his fingers — and rises. He scratches his chin, then dives for the overnight case behind the armchair, rummaging around in it until he finds his battery-powered shaver. He could shave right here in his father's room but prefers the public men's room out in the hall — it's a change of scene, at least. Ellen understands, seems to. She nods and stretches, waves him on out. Her eyes look glazed; his own must, too. They're all exhausted.

He could put in a call to the office while he's at it; they were in the midst of a personnel hassle when he left. But, then again, he doesn't know when he'll be able to get back, so what would be the point? Better leave things as they are.

Cliff is vice president of a small but upscale advertising firm in Dallas. They take on a range of freelance assignments but, for the most part, specialize in cosmetics. Unless pressed, his father never mentions to anyone else what it is Cliff does for a living. It means nothing that Cliff has risen so high and swiftly through the ranks, and done so without connections — what possible connections could he have? He's moved up by the power of his determination. By his own wits. Mental sweat is how Cliff thinks of it. All lost on his father, for whom desk work is merely "paper shuffling." And the old man has scant respect for the business of advertising; calling it, at best, "secondhand smoke," but, most of the time, "lies — plain and simple."

"He isn't the same man," Ellen had warned him when she summoned him from Dallas three days ago. But he was the same man — shrunk up, yes, but the same — exactly! Still trying to listen in on everything. Clapping one ear shut and pointing the other at you, his hearing half gone. Short on breath, maybe, but still gasping out the same old windy tales of hard times and good old times, of his cowpunching days, rolling out of bed in the cracking cold of before-dawn, of haying and calving crews. Your ear wore out eventually. That old joke about how he'd be content to live and look out from the asshole of a donkey, only to be in this world, to continue to be in the world. And on and on and on . . . a steady runoff, his voice seeping like a weepy faucet. To his dying day, he'd be the same!

To his dying day. . . . Chances were, this would be his dying day. "He can't hold out much longer," the doctor had predicted.

Cliff shaves in the men's room under harsh fluorescent light. He's inherited his father's chin, he notices for the umpteenth time, the same cleft, same aggressive thrust to it. "A chin like you've got means you're insatiable — a man to be avoided," Alisa, his girlfriend of last year, used to tease him. She specialized in reading facial features. When Cliff went to the library to check up on her sources, he found a surprising number of books on the subject, and that's exactly what they said. For whatever it was worth — He's never liked his chin.

Quick turn round the corridor. It's pretty busy this afternoon. There are kids running in and out of the playroom. Cliff collides with a toddler who's wearing a toy stethoscope round his neck. He reaches out, grabbing, trying to break the boy's fall, but misses; the swoop of his rescuing arm seems to scare the kid even more than the fall. "Mommy!" he wails. "Gonna tell on you! Maa —" One of the nurses heads towards them. Cliff starts to explain, which proves unnecessary — she saw it happening. As she bends down to soothe the boy, Cliff slips away. He still intends to make a couple rounds of the corridors before returning to his father's room.

Passing the nurses' station, he can't help overhearing the patient-nurse intercom, a bluff, hearty voice announcing: "It was just wind!" and the nurse coming back with "It was good you tried anyway, you have to keep trying." This place is really getting to Cliff. Imagine broadcasting such details!

Cliff manages to make two complete rounds of the corridors before he notices a chiming coming from the nurses' station — no one answering. Must mean they're all busy elsewhere . . . . Simply to be on the safe side, he does an abrupt about-face and returns to his father's room.

But there's nothing doing here. His mother's still sleeping, head bowed, in her chair. Ellen has gone elsewhere — probably out to the courtyard for a smoke. The old man is sputtering in what looks like uneasy sleep. One hand has a roothold on the tubing, pinching off the oxygen supply. Cliff twists it free from the clutching hand. Accidentally, he touches his father's mouth, feels the clinging moistness, shudders.

By 2:30 that afternoon the old man is entering a new phase. A forced march of breath — it's as if he's climbing, laboring ever more steeply uphill. Here and there, words can be made out: "Up the road a ways . . . ," he says, pointing, giving directions to someone only he sees. "It was running perfect," he says a little later, sounding mournful. His fingers have curled into hooks; only his mouth is moving now. He labors, yet lies there as if bound hand and foot.

Taking his father's hand in his own, Cliff feels the coldness coming on. The nurse seems to have forgotten the mask. For a brief moment, Cliff considers pushing the call button to ask why she hasn't switched, then answers his own question: because it wouldn't make any difference now.

And then the old man opens his eyes. His movement is calm,

unhurried, the expression in his eyes canny and clear; he says to no one in particular, to the air: "Tell Cliff to hold off spraying till the wind's down." It's a whisper, a fraction of a whisper, there's no body to it at all, and Cliff cannot be sure whether he actually hears this or only imagines it. Then the old man's eyes shut, as if to seal the thing said. This was no imagining. His last clear communication — Cliff already knows that it will be the last — unanswerable.

The labor of breath resumes: one long and abrasive, two smooth, short sighs, a pause, and then the breaths are scarcely divided, so thin and shapeless. He's back to his dying —

— Which goes on more quietly all through the afternoon. Cliff has moved from anger to exhaustion — he hasn't slept but three or four hours in the last two nights. Struggling to keep his head from nodding, he hears the smallest sound, like a needle ringing. Then a whispered "go see," though no one has spoken. Cliff glances round at the others: no — no one. His mother is drowsing, still in a sitting position, chin tucked into her chest. He can make out the shine of her scalp where her hair has thinned. Ellen casts a questioning gaze in Cliff's direction — did she hear it, too? There it goes again — he holds his breath.

"Go see . . ."

Something has entered: it's as if a door has silently opened and, as silently, shut. The fan continues working on high, the door he *can* see — the actual door to the courtyard — remains ajar, but there is no other wind, no sound, nothing stirring. That blasted wind — Cliff misses it! And rising before the others, he steps forward, the first to confront his father, now so strangely still.

At the Door

YESTERDAY afternoon, Hannah began dictating a long list of things needing to be taken care of, starting with *keys*. Her daughters — Ruthie and Rachel — took turns writing. The dictation dragged on and on, most of it concerning trifles. It was hard for Ruthie to keep her mind on the task at hand, so when her mother said "plants," what she wrote was "plans." When Ruthie read the list back to her, Hannah was upset, losing her train of thought. "*Plans?* What plans *could* I have?" she asked. From then on she made Ruthie double-check each and every item.

The strange part was that Ruthie had been looking at the plants on the windowsill when she failed to put down the right word — staring straight at them — for she'd forgotten to freshen the water in the vase with the carnations. The carnation petals were still brightly crimsoned, but the flowers had stopped drinking; the water in the vase, faintly clouded, rested at the same level, a bare inch under the glossy lip.

Now, morning — one more day. The list is done. Hannah is plainly exhausted, yet she's got herself so propped up by pillows — one under each shoulder, two at her head — that it looks like sitting up. She's restless, too, though she says she isn't; her eyes keep opening and shutting, her fingers roving.

And here's the latest: Hannah's sending Rachel out to "make arrangements." Those are her exact words; she's that matter-of-fact about it — that *cold*. Her mother's speech is slurred, but Ruthie, who has only stepped out for a breather, hasn't missed a thing. And that overheard "arrangements" stops her dead in her tracks right outside the door. Has Rachel felt it, too? She must have, for now Hannah's trying to soften the word by adding, "It's for *my* peace of mind. *You're* the practical one, Rachel." Nothing new in this. Send Ruthie out for a loaf of bread and she'll climb a tree is the way the story goes. It's one of those family stories.

Hannah promises to be here when Rachel returns and will do her very best. (Not all promises can be kept, of course.) Rachel steps out of the room hiding tears, her head bent, too hurt to answer her mother, or even to glance at Ruthie. Ruthie is left with the distinct impression that whatever's going to happen will be between her mother and herself, just the two of them.

The plain truth is — Hannah's too tired to be tactful this morning, and Rachel has been making her jittery with all her fussing, her continual fluffing of pillows and smoothing of sheets. Pestering her with questions: would she like this, would she like that? It makes no difference, this or that. Hannah, herself, has never been demonstrative, never worn her heart on her sleeve — it has to be pried out of hiding. In this, she's like her younger daughter, Ruthie. Hannah knows that Ruthie is there, standing only inches from the door, but she isn't about to summon Ruthie to her side; she wouldn't even if she did have the breath for it. Nobody can force Ruthie: she'll have to move on her own prompting.

With Rachel, it's a clash of different temperaments. With Ruthie it's the opposite: no clash, but a continual, silent pulling away. Hannah and Ruthie are too much alike, too close for comfort, they know too much about each other. Seems like it's always been this way, though there were years — Ruthie's terrible teens — when they couldn't speak face to face without a blowup, and Hannah was forced to communicate by passing notes under her daughter's bedroom door. It was Hannah who knew exactly when Ruthie's first crush started. She didn't know the name of the boy for sure, but she was confident that, somewhere, buried deeply in a mess of loose-leaf papers, was a sheet tattered with too much handling and, on it, *his* name written over and over, filling all the lines, even the unlined margins. Ruthie never confided, but Hannah *knew*. And it was Hannah, again, who was the first to suspect that her daughter's marriage had turned sour, months before Ruthie would even begin to admit it to herself. Theirs is a mutual attunement; it works in the other direction as well; Ruthie has often — too often for her liking — found herself completing her mother's sentences in midcourse. This happens on all subjects, not simply nags.

Nothing hurts Hannah anymore. She's simply so very tired. Her indwelling catheter dangles loosely, like a tassel, over her collarbone, an irritation when she thinks about it. Her twisting and turning keeps dislodging the tape that holds the catheter in place. The device ought to have been pulled when she was admitted, but there was too much going on, and, anyway, it won't be long. Around Hannah, the world still looks festive: the curtains are open, and there's a golden willow directly in her line of vision: a small tree, still unleafed, but its arms are gleaming orange, it looks incandescent. The morning is clear and cloudless; Hannah's drinking in the light, the last sips. The last time she tasted actual food was days back — a few spoonfuls of lukewarm broth — nothing she'd ever miss.

Two crossings yet to go, Hannah thinks. Alone. Even if Ruthie decides to come back in, I'm on my own. The first crossing will be familiar, she reasons; she's been navigating it all her life, night after night, moving trustingly into sleep, and from sleep into dreams. The dreams are lighted and can be tracked; only the boundary remains dark, the place where all forgetting starts. The second crossing would be like the first — darker, but not foreign, not utterly strange. Hannah tries to picture what cannot be pictured. She imagines a slow dissolve, an underwater space, brightness and shade, dim lights spotting the bottom of the sea, floating and fading. . . . She tells herself she is not afraid.

Ruthie continues to stand outside the room, close to the partway open door. She keeps peeking in, although only the foot of the bed and the visitor's armchair can be glimpsed through the opening. If smoking were permitted, she'd light up, it would give her an excuse for standing where she does, but her hands are idle — she has no excuse. She doesn't allow herself to lean against the wall but stands stiffly apart from everything. "A picture of stage fright" one of the nurses will caption it later, when they talk the day over, and the two others who happen to observe Ruthie will agree. Stage fright is only part of the picture, though.

Motionless, her eyes roaming, Ruthie is ready to fasten on any distraction. At the moment, it's scraps of the conversation going on at the nurses' station; she can catch most of it, enough to know it's about food, about this patient who won't give up food. He's on a nasogastric pump, can't taste, swallow, or digest, but still he wants his meals. "It's the *idea* of food he can't let go of —" Somebody's bed check is shrilling. The nurses all hurry off in the direction of the alarm: a patient who shouldn't be moving must be wandering loose from his bed.

But — what's the solution? Ruthie wonders. Maybe there isn't any. Even if she waits here all day, the story may never be resumed. So why doesn't she move?

It's the idea of death she can't swallow. Here she's traveled all the way from Atlanta to be with her mother and, at the crunch, cannot bring herself to enter the room. Instead, she persists in standing on the threshold — half in, half out — like a word formed, but arrested, on the lips. The word could be *fear,* it could be *anger.* It could be *love.* When she spies one of the chattier volunteers heading her way, Ruthie tries to ward her off by thrusting her palm up like a traffic cop, and then, abruptly, turning her back on the woman, staring off to the far end of the corridor, to the glass door where no one is entering. She blinks — a cascade of blinkings, telling her what a strain her stillness has been. It occurs to Ruthie how rarely her mother blinks now. A small change, by itself, but added to so many others. . . . Another reason Ruthie shouldn't wait. It's no use, though — thoughts, reasons, they don't change anything. And so she continues to stand there, mind racing a mile a minute, legs frozen, glued to the spot. She doesn't much like herself at this moment. But she's trying, really, she is.

Ruthie can't blame herself — not entirely. It's all been so unexpected: she needs more time to take it in. At least nobody can accuse her of failing to respond quickly enough. After Rachel called with her terrible news, within the same hour, Ruthie had canceled her office appointments for the week, arranged for her daughter, Kit, to be picked up by her other grandmother, and reserved a seat on the earliest flight out. Getting Kit ready, by itself, was no small feat: she'd stalled by throwing herself on the floor. Lay there like a sack of meal. No tears — nothing but implacable stubbornness. Ruthie argued in vain, made promises, offered bribes, and, finally, did consent to stop everything and search for the tiny teddy bear belonging to Kit's sleep doll — her doll's doll — which Kit refused to leave without. This involved turning the room upside down. Then, moving the bed out, Ruthie discovered the graffiti on the bedroom wall: the name KIT in red Magic Marker that couldn't be wiped off. Ruthie was furious at first, then repentant, haunted by it. Kit was six, old enough to be aware of parents quarreling, well able to connect this with Ruthie's deciding to move them out of the house and into an apartment. And it didn't take much imagination for Ruthie to grasp that Kit's making a record of her name was her way of snatching a little bit of permanence from a shiftless world.

Already frazzled with that leave-taking, Ruthie had arrived in time to be part of her mother's transfer from hospital to hospice. Together, Rachel, Ruthie, and one of the student nurses had wheeled Hannah over, across the glassed-in walkway bridging the buildings. The crossing took only a moment, yet it felt like ages. What it really felt like was the passage to another world. The bridge was at treetop level, its long windows dusky with the first feathering leaves of the season. Below her, Ruthie saw people and cars moving; a family picnicking on the hospital lawn; a brown-spotted dog lifting a leg, pissing against a tire; the world went on. "Looks festive," her mother said, following Ruthie's gaze. She actually said that — "festive."

Ruthie had sneaked a glance at the social worker's report before they'd started over. The summing-up was dry and professional: *Patient understands her limited life expectancy....* Understands far too well, Ruthie suspected, and probably the reason her mother had refused to be wheeled over in a hospital bed or gurney as the nurses had recommended. Instead, her mother had insisted upon sitting up in a wheelchair. She could still sit on her own then, although she kept sagging. *There are no unmet needs at this time. . . .* Ruthie's mother held tightly to the possessions in her lap, all she would ever need at this, or any, time: comb and brush, cup, tooth swabs, a cake of soap, and a small, kidney-shaped, basin — they filled a pink plastic tub, not much bigger than a bread box.

Hannah had already given her garnet ring to Rachel and her watch to Ruthie, but she seemed to forget about the watch and, every now and then, waiting for the hospice admission procedure to begin, Ruthie would catch her consulting her empty wrist. It was hard, Ruthie guessed, to put aside such an old habit as time.

The wait for the admitting nurse was long, and it had been Ruthie, not her mother, who'd broken down. "You're only fifty-one, Ma!" she'd blurted. She could have kicked herself, it was nothing she'd ever planned to say — the words simply flew out of her. Turned out, her mother knew everything. It was she who tried to console Ruthie: "It's not how many years, it's the unlived life in them that gets you in the end. I've lived my life every minute. There's nothing to regret." She spoke the words chin up, eyes focused on Ruthie. Her speech was still sharp then — unwavering and clear.

Although she gave no sign of it, Hannah, too, caught herself wondering, even as she was speaking. Was it true what she was saying? Or did it only seem true now, the death of desire preceding the death of the body, flattening the ground and easing the way? Surely, it hadn't always been true. Naturally, there had been moments when. . . . A musical career set aside when she married, for a start. And she could go on from there. Of course she'd never have made concert grade; marriage had saved her from any delusions of grandeur on that score. And on the whole, taken as a whole — Why did she shake her head right then? Had Ruthie noticed? But no, she wasn't sorry. No.

Ruthie balked as she listened. Why did this feel like betrayal? The false upbeat — no doubt meant to project reassurance — clashed with everything she knew and remembered. It was as if she and her mother hadn't been living in the same house, the same story. *No regrets?* How could she? Dad walking out on them when Ruthie was five, then disappearing for good when the divorce came through. No support. Zilch. That was before the days you could hunt runaway fathers down. Her mother a workhorse from then on, never remarrying. How could she pretend her life was complete? Her good piano, the centerpiece of their living room, never sold but no longer played, no longer tuned. No regrets, huh? How? Who was she trying to fool?

After that little oration, Ruthie couldn't believe how quickly her mother started going downhill. The nursing staff established what they called a breakthrough dose on the medication right away — breaking through the pain — a real success there. Then, in the promptness of their follow-ups, it seemed like they were trying to erase not only the pain but the very memory of pain, then — memory, itself. And maybe they'd even slipped in a mood brightener on the side — how else account for her mother's almost eager compliance?

Today would be her mother's fourth day at hospice. There'd been no further words of wisdom in the intervening time. All that was granted were those few decent hours on the afternoon of the transfer when her mother said she was "acclimating" — she always preferred the fancier words — then the slide began. By the next morning, she started to sound toothless, as though she were gumming things — the words not separate, not sharp.

Deep down, Ruthie couldn't help feeling that her mother didn't *have* to give in this soon if she put her mind to it — if she loved life enough to fight like hell for it.

The nurses thought Hannah was doing as well as could be, though. "She's a real sweetie," they kept on telling Ruthie. It was easy enough to translate what "sweetie" meant to them: she didn't complain, didn't give them a whole lot of work. But when one of the nurses confided, "She's a true angel," Ruthie couldn't connect it with the mother she remembered.

Her mother had worked time and overtime to keep up the house payments, and was usually cranky and distracted by the time she got home. "Angel" didn't fit her character at all. She'd been dutiful and distracted. Ruthie had wanted a mom like most of her friends — and all of the magazines — had back in those days. Somebody who'd be there, rested and smiling, welcoming her home from school with snacks waiting, the table set, waxed floors shining, the whole house gleaming spick-and-span. Instead, by the time Rachel was ten and Ruthie seven, it was up to the two of them to get supper warmed and on the table. And what suppers! Tuna Helper, Hamburger Helper, instant macaroni and cheese, stews that were made to last and last by adding water on the third day. The only time the house looked even halfway decent was after Saturday laundry and vacuuming; waxing was a sometime luxury. Ruthie had wanted a mother with time to play. Instead, she and Rachel had been hurried through their weekends. Hurried through their illnesses — no lazing around at home watching shows on television after the fever was down. No coddling — her mother had never been one for that, or, if she had, it was too far back for Ruthie ever to recall it.

But Ruthie is twenty-eight now; her daughter, Kit, will soon be starting in on her own reckoning. Ruthie, too, is about to be divorced; and she, too, works — she's a landscape architect. It's a real career, competitive and demanding. Coming at the end of a long working day, Ruthie and Kit's suppers have been the easiest: endless spaghetti and, yes, stews in the Crock-Pot in quantities ample enough for a second day and more. They've also eaten their share of send-out pizzas, Chinese takeouts, even TV dinners — all the shortcuts. Ruthie, herself, hasn't been the most attentive of mothers. . . . But the past is done-for, the present almost done-for — *Now's* the moment, now if ever . . . Ruthie cannot banish the images: the way her mother's fingers seemed to be playing scales over the rumpled sheets, the narrow glint of eye white, the soft, glubbing noises she made as she moved in and out of sleep.

Ruthie sighs, squares her shoulders, commands herself — *don't waste another second. Move it!* — and turns. Poises one foot in front of the other. She's ready. But again pauses on the threshold, touching her left hand to the plaque with the room number and to her mother's name, *Hannah Mosher,* Magic-Markered in bright blue beneath. The name is written in cursive, a single, twisting line: the letters are unbraiding, slowly, right before her eyes. All Ruthie can do is stare at it. Stare, and stand there. Can't budge.

Hannah's fading, in and out. She knows that Ruthie's close by, just outside, still unable to enter. "Don't worry" — she starts to tell her, but hasn't the breath, and finishes the sentence to herself — *it's all level from here on out.* Then: *Oh, wait — one more thing* — and has already forgotten what it was.

Where was she? . . . Alone. On the way. Woozy, little bit lost and . . .

. . . finds herself at home, closing up for the night. She walks the hall slowly, turns off lights as she goes. It is so quiet. In the whole house, she's the only one awake. Sees a door partway open onto a room she never knew existed. All these years — how come she's missed it? Inside: a table set for three, a break-front, sparkling crystal, her great-aunt's scroll-back chairs. The room glows, the table gleams and beckons. She wants to ask, *all right if I?* — but knows she can't go in. Enter — and she'd wake up forever, turn away — she'd never find it again. All she can do is stand there, gazing in —

Spring Me

W HAT are those pretty ones called?" Louellen
pointed.

"I'm not real sure. Gladys-something."

"Oh no, those pinkish white ones are glads — they're the
only ones I recognize.

Louellen White and Olive Masters were on "flower patrol."
Olive worked on housekeeping mostly, but she had an artis-
tic flair, was always rearranging flowerpots, lamps, and chairs
for a better effect, and, anyway, nobody else could be spared,
so she was a natural for the job. Louellen was the least senior member of the nursing team, so she got conscripted. The
wreaths and floral baskets kept coming in from the funeral
homes, piling up in the receiving room, and they were driving
Sharon, who happened to be a unit manager today, nearly
crazy. Only last month, Sharon had lost her baby sister,
Annie — so, whenever she saw a big floral spread, it put her in
mind of that, and she'd walk around muttering "tear it up!"
not quite under her breath, until someone overheard her and
got with it. Then, whoever it was who got stuck with the
assignment would divide up the best flowers, stick them in bud
vases, and take them round to the rooms.

If dismantling funeral wreaths was going to become one of her regular assignments, Louellen thought she might as well go on ahead and quit. It was the least favorite thing she'd had to do so far — she'd rather empty bedpans, at least you knew what was what. Louellen still couldn't say how she felt about working here, it changed so much from minute to minute, and whenever anyone asked her where she was working now, she only named the hospital — hospice being too much to explain.

"How do you like this one?" Olive put forward one of the finished bud vases: glads and carnation and fern.

"Real pretty," Louellen said.

"You're just saying that."

"No, it's nice. I mean it."

The spread they turned to next was one of the harder ones. The flowers — red and white carnations — were arranged, some long, some short, to shape a heart. Not a real heart, of course, but a heart like in valentines. Their stems were angled into a green sponge; they had short, daggerlike spikes clamped to the ends. Louellen noticed, for the first time, how the taller flowers were wired the length of their stems, green wires going all the way up to where the blossoms started, piercing the delicate green cups that bound the petals.

Neither Olive nor Louellen had a whole lot more to say about the flowers.

"I think Katie's off the program. Tuning out," Olive ventured.

"I kinda wondered, myself," said Louellen

Katie was in 115; she was the longest-lived patient on the unit. Only a month back, the popular prediction had been that she'd outlast everybody on the staff. Louellen, who was still new and brought a fresh outlook to things, didn't agree. Even in the few weeks since she'd started to work at hospice, she could see the fading. Katie had pretty much stopped eating;

lately, when she saw a tray coming at her, she was likely to say, "Chicken today — feathers tomorrow!" and turn up her nose at it, whether it was chicken or not. She still kept up her Tuesday manicure, pedicure, and hair set, at her daughter's insisting, was still elegant even down to her glossy red toenails, but last Tuesday, right after she'd been prettied up, she'd whispered to Louellen, "Pray for my release." If that wasn't a tip-off, Louellen didn't know what was.

"I caught her waving the other day," said Olive. "You know how that goes — waving and greeting? The dead husband taps at the window or waves from the doorway, but doesn't come in unless you're really close to the end." Louellen thought that might be it: Katie had mentioned that her husband stopped by in the mornings while she was still in bed; she seemed to have forgotten that she'd been a widow for years.

"We don't see what they see," Olive said softly.

Louellen must have sighed or something, because Olive quickly added, "You can't let it get you down," and launched right into a pep talk. "What you've got to appreciate," she said, "is that most everybody coming in here gets quality time. Some of them get to feeling better than they've felt in months. Years, sometimes. And a bunch of them get to go home. There was this little old lady in 104, right before you came — she left here to live it up in Vegas. Her time remaining hadn't changed, far as anybody could see, but the way she felt about it sure took a turn. You know what I'm saying?"

Olive wasn't used to making speeches, and it showed; she lapsed into silence when she was done. Louellen busied herself gathering up all the flowers they'd rejected, the wilted and the straggly ones.

Then Olive piped up with a new theme. Out of the blue — "And what's *your* story?" she asked.

"What d'you mean — 'story'?" Louellen stood there, hands full of stems, and stared at Olive.

"Everybody has one," Olive explained, "especially people who end up working here. Especially the volunteers, didn't you know that? Cora lost a husband — right here on the unit, couple years back. You can't work on the floor the first year, but you can after that if they think you've got a grip on your grieving. Pat lost a kid, I think in a hospital out of state. Jim McBride had cancer and came to work here after he'd been free of it for five years — he made a promise to the Lord. It was his way of saying thank you."

"First of all, I'm not a volunteer — I'm an LVN, a fully licensed vocational nurse," Louellen reminded her.

"Oh, I know that," Olive said, "but you know."

Louellen, who didn't like telling everybody her business, turned the tables on Olive then. "What's *your* story?" she asked.

"All right, sure," Olive said, as she freed a speckled white and red carnation from its dagger. "I don't mind going first."

"Fertile Myrtle, that's me," she began. "Seven kids and would of been more. My mom had sixteen — can you believe it? Four didn't make it. All my dad had to do was to look at her and she'd have another one. So she bought him a television. Wasn't as easy for Dick and me, though. Dick can only set so long. I was about ready to get my tubes tied when I got the change instead. Dick was still driving me up the wall, though. You know how that goes . . ." She glanced at Louellen for some sort of comeback, but Louellen only shrugged. "The thing is, Dick's semiretired now, see. He works as a greeter at Walmart twenty hours a week — that still leaves too many hours with him at home and time on his hands. And no money coming in. So I decided it was time to get myself up and out of the house . . ."

It went on like this; Louellen sort of tuned out — not delib-
erate, a drifting. There'd simply been too many words to the
hour today. She wasn't used to it.

Then Olive's voice trailed off; she stared at Louellen. Her
turn now.

"Well . . . if it's a story, it sure is a short one," Louellen
began. "Like I said, I'm an LVN. And married seventeen years.
My husband just upped and walked out on me one day. I saw
an ad in the paper and I came to work here. That's about it."

"That's a bunch," said Olive. "Was there another woman?
You don't mind my asking?"

"Look, I don't feel —"

"I don't want to pry, honey," said Olive. "But his walking
out doesn't mean you're a bad person. You've got to keep
telling yourself that. And that you've got a right to be happy."

"I really don't think there was another woman. Leastways,
he hasn't hooked up with anybody yet. He just got tired of
being married. It happens, I guess . . ."

"Isn't *this* pretty?" Olive said. She held up a bunch of baby's
breath. "I always liked baby's breath." She could see that
Louellen was close to tears. "Maybe a jot of it here — what
d'ya think?" Olive crowded the baby's breath into a bud vase
that was pretty full already. Louellen didn't comment one way
or the other. "Advice is cheap, I know," Olive went on, "and I'm
ten years your senior, if a day. Let me tell you something —"

"Shoot," said Louellen.

"I'm not too smart, myself, but you've heard the goings-on
in 106?"

Louellen nodded.

"Seen that six-year-old in 101?"

"Actually, I think she's eight or nine — she's very tiny,"
Louellen corrected.

"Eight, nine, or twenty-two, it's *really* sad. Kinda makes you wonder. Thing like that cuts other things down to size."

Louellen sighed. "Sure is sad," she agreed.

"Anyway, what I was saying was: live all you can while you can. Eat it all up, every bit that's coming to you, hon. Anybody offer it — you reach for it, both hands. See that fellow?" Olive pointed her scissor blades at the door.

Louellen craned her neck to see. "Wonder if he knows where he's *at?*" she mused.

A shriveled-up old man was wobbling down the corridor, singing as he went. He was wearing a ten-gallon hat and cracked, mud-rusted boots. His voice was parched.

It was no song Louellen had ever heard. Something about a "big, bald man" — or maybe a "big-balled man." She couldn't even recognize the tune.

"Gonna find me a woman . . . someday," he sang. Strange words, but the rest was a lost as he rounded the bend on the north side.

"Looks like he's had a few already." Louellen smiled.

"Quite a few," said Olive.

It's the weekend shift, inching along to Saturday night on the high lonesome plains of Texas, everybody antsy to be up and going and doing. What tires Olive most is the fact — the mere *thought* — of so many different things going on at the same exact minute, each room a little world. In 104, they're celebrating a wedding anniversary — somebody's fortieth. In 105, the patient is getting a suppository. In 106, everything's over: the young man there had been terribly restless for days before the end — his fidgeting hands and feet already the color of slate. His parents had done their best not to let on that he was dying. When — much too late — he asked straight out, his mother could only whisper, "Yes, honey, you are," and her tears said everything. "What do I do? What do I do? Hold my breath?" he'd struggled to sit up. "I don't know, hon" — more tears. Finally, he closed his eyes and let his hands slip; everything seemed to be taking care of itself. His mother was standing up to fetch a nurse, when, at that very instant, he roused himself out of what looked like coma, pleading with more voice than anybody could *believe,* "Don't let me die!" — and promptly died. His last words. His parents were beside themselves, and even the staff was a bit shaken. The family's gone now, and the young man's room seems emptier than empty. But, Olive reminds herself, she hasn't any time to linger: they're expecting a transfer from the hospital any minute now. The new patient is to go in 109. With the unit so full and the nursing staff so stretched and stressed, Olive has her work cut out for her. She cleans but also listens for the intercom, attends and fetches, does whatever she can do to save the nurses a few steps.

In 109, Olive vacuums and dusts, replacing the plastic liner in the trash basket and elevating the bed; she lifts the wick in the bottle of industrial air freshener — it's strong lemon — the strongest of any kind she's worked with, though it can't hide everything. She sets the bottle down on the shelf near the bed. For good measure, she sends a few spritzes of piney-scented household spray towards the ceiling, aiming a triple blast in the general direction of the visitors' couch. She checks for toilet paper and soap in the bathroom — all in order — then wheels the cart out.

Near the end of the hall, in 114, there's a preacher standing by the window, reciting Scripture. Olive can't make out the particular words, but she knows it's a preacher by how loud he whispers. Is he the one who did the baptism in the whirlpool bath that everyone goes on and on about? In Olive's book, that famous last-minute baptism was taking advantage. There are some things you don't ask, but she often wonders: is she the only one who doesn't think it was a perfectly wonderful thing to do?

What *really* gets Olive's goat is something one of the preachers did last year — she hasn't seen him since — trying to pray the cancer out of a lady's liver, telling her it was a testing of her faith; if her faith was strong enough, her tumor would shrivel in its radiating force. That's the man Olive's on the lookout for. After he'd left, Olive stopped in to visit with the lady and to toss in her own two cents: "There are other kinds of healing, you know." The patient knew: "I let him carry on," she confided, "so's not to hurt his feelings."

Even at the end, people tended to be polite. Really gracious, considering . . . All but a few, Olive thinks. And speaking of the devil —

There goes the emergency bell — it's 111, Billy Blakely. It would be. Up to his old mischief.

She parks her cart close to the wall and hoofs it, empty-handed, down the corridor. Barges through the door, shooting off her mouth even before she's taken a good look: "Who's being ugly here?"

He doesn't bother to reply. Olive sees at once what he's done, he's done it before — ripped the call button unit out of the wall. She picks it up, plugs it back in — it's easy enough to reattach — but what a rumpus when it's pulled! The bell ceases.

"Somebody trying to say something here?" she reframes the question.

"You old hornet, you!" Billy greets her.

*　　*　　*

Olive does her best to contain herself. *Look at you* — she says under her breath — *nothing but a great big adolescent, and pushing fifty, I bet.* Would she tolerate Billy for one minute if he were well? The answer is sadly clear: not for a minute.

Billy's sitting and smoking in his wheelchair, ashtray balanced on his empty footrest, the wheelchair angled for a quick getaway out the door. His red hair is dark with damp or oil, slicked flat, carefully parted. Olive can't help admiring how dolled up he looks, all ready for a night on the town. Sure has got his stuffing back. But where's he off to? With boots? Hat? His hat sits at the ready, perched on his lap, one of those really good Resistol ones, black, with a nice crown crease and a smiling brim. And he's wearing jeans, a belt with a big silver rodeo buckle. His plaid shirt's got pearly snap buttons, but he's canceled out the fanciness of that by rolling his sleeves up to show off his tattoos. There's one on each arm: a Texas map with the lone star and a longhorn in the middle of it; the other, an Air Force insignia. Got a two-tone black and yellow snakeskin boot on his one foot. Other side: the jean leg's folded neatly, safety-pinned at the knee.

"Going someplace?" Olive asks.

"Checking out," Billy puffs: a perfect O. He's waiting, he says, on one of his buddies from the packing plant. "And now I'd appreciate it if you'd kindly fuck off," he says quietly, pausing before he adds, "ma'am."

"No I won't," says Olive. "You can't take off as you please. You have to wait on your nurse to check you out. Barbara is your nurse, isn't she?"

Billy shrugs; names don't mean much to him, that's clear. He's down to the nub of his present cigarette, so now he uses it to light up a new one. And, sure, they're filterless, it doesn't make a particle of difference by now.

"There's a regular checkout routine, you know?" Olive keeps on. "Medications checked out and such."

Billy makes a big blowing sound. "Dammit! I've done the routine. She signed me out. I've got my shit together — I'm done already." He points to the couch, where a paper sack with his meds in it and a bunch of papers have been tossed. "I'm outta here. Up and gone. Gone —" he all but sings it. "Waiting for Randy to get here, is all."

"Mind if I ask your plans?"

"Honky-tonking — all night long." Billy gives Olive a most radiant smile. "Gonna live it up tonight!" And he flexes one withered arm to show where the bulge of muscle used to be. "Dancing! Can't be fancy dancing — slow dancing it'll hafta be —"

Dancing? A one-legged man? Olive has her doubts about that. Maybe if he does take it slow and easy, he can move to the music in his wheelchair, or follow a partner, the right partner. . . . He's pretty adept with those wheels. And he's all pumped up tonight.

He's reviewing it and reviewing it before he's even out the door. "Gonna stop at ever' blessed honkey-tonk on the boulevard — Hitching Post, Red River Roundup, Crystal Pistol, Flying Spur — Gonna get me a squeeze tonight! Yessiree . . ."

Olive remembers Billy Blakely from the hour he first came in. That was three, four months back, when Billy still had a wife. A visible wife, that is. They were at it all the time, tooth and tong, scrapping every minute, but the lady stuck with him. They might, even now, still be married for all Olive knew. All kinds of marrieds in this world. But the wife hasn't shown her face, not once, this second round, and Billy has been in for over a week.

From the first, Billy made his mark as one of the meanest

patients in the history of the unit. "He's too mean to die!" Olive let loose the day after his admission, the words leaping from her lips, after he'd torn up his room twice in a couple of hours.

With Billy there was never a quiet moment: he hollered for booze, he hollered for the Playboy Channel, he spent most of his time giving grief to his wife, and he was happy to lay it on anybody else who dared to cross him. The fact of having one leg gone to cancer from the knee down hadn't slowed him like it was supposed to do. Plus, he still had plenty of power in that left paw of his — he was a lefty — and he loved to throw things. So he moved around all the time and even got himself to the toilet on his own, hurling himself from bed to wheelchair in a kind of fury. Wouldn't even consider a bedside commode. Normal underwear was too hard to manage, and he sure as hell wasn't about to wear a Foley catheter or a paper diaper.

Olive recalled one of those bathroom sessions. She'd been in the room with the wife and the nurse struggling to help Billy out of bed. How angry he'd been! His gown was too short, and he'd rucked it up shorter, and his wife rushed to find a towel and drape it over him, saying with a kind of glee: "Have a fig leaf, dear!" And how Billy threw the towel off in cussed, shaming defiance. Olive marveled at how much red blood was still beating through there.

"Lez get outta here!" Randy's barely darkened the doorway and Billy's raring to be off.

"Grab up those papers, will ya? And that sack" — he points — "and that duffel over there, and this pile of laundry here." That's how Billy greets Randy, his hand darting all over the place.

"Hold your horses, man," Randy says. He looks the stuff

over and decides it's going to take two trips — one for the gear, another for the wheelchair. Billy insists he can handle the wheelchair himself, but Olive butts in arguing: why not save that energy for dancing? She volunteers to wait with Billy till Randy returns, and tries to make a joke of it, saying Billy's liable to fly up out of his chair. It's no joke, though — Billy's smooshed, face flushed, hot already just thinking about tonight.

"Don't know what you folks have been giving him," Randy says, "but whatever it is, can I have some, too?"

Billy lights up another cigarette while he waits. Buzzing to himself like a live wire all the while, one arm drumming on the armrest while he chants: "Yessir . . . gonna hit the Crystal Pistol tonight. Live it up tonight! Gonna have me a big time — *quality time!*"

Olive recognizes "quality time" as one of their own well-worn hospice slogans, but it strikes her that Billy's version of it might not be exactly what the founder had in mind.

Now Randy's back. "Guess that about winds it up," he says, releasing the wheelchair brakes and launching Billy, "time to get this show on the road." Billy bends to stub out his cigarette, handing the ashtray to Randy, who hands it over to Olive.

Olive gives Billy one of her friendliest pats, a hearty double clump on the shoulder. "Be careful," she almost blurts, but bites it back in time. *Spend it, spend it,* she wishes him under her breath. Out loud, she wishes him well in the usual way. She wonders whether she'll see him again, how much time he's got.

Then Billy, surprising Olive, blows her a kiss, tossing it over his shoulder as he goes. He's still spouting as he rides through the door: "Oh, a honey!"

II

Trying to See

Moment to Moment

THEY were being good; their mother only had to tell them once about not throwing the Smurf ball into the hallway where big people might trip over it. The two children were sitting on the floor with a pile of toys between them. One, then the other, kept going to the shelves and bringing down some new thing, although there were plenty of toys on the floor already.

After only a few minutes Jeff wanted to quit. "Let's go back in the room," he said.

"Don't be a baby — we can't go in now," Lindsey reminded him. "They're taking the gadgets out of Granpa."

"I want to see Granpa go to heaven," said Jeff, and his face got very red.

"You can't *see* that," Lindsey said. "He's going to go in a box. They have to send him."

"*Who* sends?" Jeff wanted to know.

Lindsey wasn't sure, but she answered as if she knew perfectly well: "The preacher, silly! Lookit this —" It was a toy wristwatch — you could set the hands. Lindsey moved the big hand to twelve and the little hand to four. Then she changed the little hand back to three, then to one, then to eleven. It was fun making time go backwards. Jeff wanted to play with the watch, too. Lindsey gave it to him because she saw something even better.

It was the play money. There were hundreds and hundreds of dollars in a basket. They were in ones and tens and fives. So many ones!

Jeff spoke in his smallest voice: "I want to sit on you," but Lindsey, bent over the basket, did not look up from her counting. Jeff wanted to go where the rest of the family was, but he wasn't sure how to get there. When he stood up and peeked into the hallway, he saw a room with an open door across from him. It had towels and sheets folded up on shelves. And Band-Aids — big ones. He saw a bowl of hair laying on top of a table in the room. It was brown — and it was curly! It looked like a lady's head when she gets her hair fixed, but there was no head inside the hair, no face, only an empty bowl where the head was supposed to be.

Lindsey looked up. "What are you staring at?"

Jeff pointed.

Then Lindsey told Jeff what a wig was and why it was curly. "Somebody got her hair fixed," she explained, "then she must of forgot."

"Why — forgot?" Jeff asked, turning away from the door.

Lindsey didn't bother to answer. So Jeff asked: "Why did the man have a bird nest on his head?" He'd asked her this before: Lindsey knew he was talking about the statue near Granpa's room — and it wasn't a birds' nest, but it was too long a story to start. Anyway, at that moment, Jeff spotted the toy dump truck parked behind the Lincoln Logs.

It was a nice enough day, the sky overcast, though they could use the moisture. Amy, the children's mother, was standing outside the back entrance, leaning against the brick wall, when Louellen passed her on her way to the pharmacy. The pharmacy was across the street, in the basement of the hospital. Louellen recognized Amy as the daughter of the new admission.

Amy was standing in the same place, still staring, when Louellen came by on her return trip. It looked as if she hadn't moved a muscle. Louellen decided she had to say something.

"How's it going?" she asked.

"Oh, all right . . . I guess," Amy replied. But clearly it wasn't. "I told the others I needed to step out for a smoke, and I didn't even bring my cigarettes, didn't even *think* of bringing them. Makes a lot of sense, right?" She started to laugh at herself, then swallowed and breathed out, so you could hear it. Louellen was about to reach over and touch Amy's shoulder. She hesitated, though, waiting for some sign of permission; she still wasn't used to all the easy patting and hugging that went on at hospice.

When she was able to look up again, Amy forced a smile. "I'll be all right," she said. "It's just that they're pulling out the tubes right now. Right this very minute . . . You know, the IV he came with from the county hospital? The doctor says it's making him worse. Adds to his swelling . . ." Her voice trailed away.

Louellen could think of nothing to say to this. It didn't matter, though, Amy went right on — talking to herself, really. "What I can't stand is: he's awake, and everything. I can't stand that."

"How's your dad taking it?"

"Oh, he accepts it. Don't ask me how! Says he's ready. But I'm not —" Again that loud swallowing. "I'll never be ready to let him go."

"Those your kids in the playroom?" Louellen asked.

Amy nodded.

"They sure looked busy. Playing away," said Louellen.

"Quietly, I hope."

"I wouldn't worry about it."

"I'll get back to them in a minute," Amy promised. "I can see it. I bet Lindsey's ruling the roost, even here. She was born to dominate. Born with a look on her face like somebody saying: 'I'm here — now everything can begin!'" Amy brightened at the recollection. "That child thinks she's hung the moon."

They fell into silence then and, not knowing what else to say, Louellen thought she ought to get moving. But Amy started up again. "Kids help a lot," she said, "at times like this, but there won't ever again be anybody like my father. The new doesn't cancel out the old."

"No," Louellen agreed, "no, it doesn't."

It was a real dump truck Jeff had found. It was neat — you could put things in it, like pieces of a jigsaw puzzle or play money, and then you could dump them; there was a thingamajig you had to push on the side of it, and the back lifted up.

The toys were in a jumble. Lindsey thought there might be a Barbie doll hidden away on one of the doll shelves but, if there was, it was too lost for her to ever find it. She found a coloring book, though, and some broken crayons. She wanted to color the page with the dragon, but she couldn't find any good dragon colors, no reds for the fire from his fire-breathing nostrils, only the green for his back. Most of the crayons were broken, and all of the best colors were gone.

What could she do with green, yellow, brown, and blue? Lindsey decided to color the page that said "Inside a Seed." It showed a seed cut down the middle. There were three arrows going into the seed, naming the parts. The arrow going into the sack in the middle said "Food." Lindsey thought she would color that yellow. It was a big space to fill, so she decided to do that part last. The edge of the sack, she lined in brown. The arrow that pointed to the edge said "Coat." Lindsey thought that was funny, to call the skin a coat. Coloring with the brown crayon was so boring.

Inside the brown coat, inside the sack of food she hadn't colored yet, was a snake with two heads, curled up tight. The arrow going to it said "Little Plant." This was the best part of the picture. Lindsey colored it green. She was most careful with the little plant. On the tips she put just a little tickle of blue. It was her best work.

Jeff had dumped out the puzzle pieces and the play money in the corner near Lindsey. Now he was loading the back of the dump truck with a bunny, a fuzzy duck, and a teddy bear. Jeff couldn't do coloring books because he made the colors spill over the lines.

Lindsey picked out another coloring book without finishing the one she started. She needed a picture she could do with green, yellow, brown, and blue. She found one with baby bears jumping in fall leaves. She could make the leaves brown and some of them yellow. The grass could still be green. This wasn't as good as the dragon would've been but better anyway than the dumb seed.

Jeff was on his knees, pushing the nose of the truck with one hand. His mouth was open, trying to make motor noises. Suddenly he stopped. With both hands, he threw the fuzzy duck out of the back of the truck. "Pop-pop-pop goes the duck!" he said. Then he made the back of the truck slant up and down. Down slid the bunny and the teddy bear. "All dead!" he let out with a shriek. "Dead!"

"Boy, are you ever dumb —!" Lindsey shouted back,

forgetting everything she'd been told about keeping her voice down. "Toys don't die — they aren't alive! You have to be *alive* before you can get to be dead. Everybody knows that!"

Dr. Perry was leaving their grandfather's room. The nurse followed, wheeling the IV pole. She got away quickly but the doctor couldn't. The family was waiting in a huddle outside the door wanting to know what to expect next. The doctor told them it was no longer a question of weeks but of days or hours. The family wanted to know whether it was all right to go back in.

"I don't see why not," the doctor said, "he should be more comfortable now."

The family started back into the room.

Amy was on her way there, too, stopping first at the playroom. She stood at the door, shaking her head at the mess. Tidying up would have to wait for later, though. She saw the doctor coming down the hall. "All clear now," he said and waved to her.

"C'mon" — Amy turned back to the children — "let's go. Don't you want to see Grandpa? Jeff?" Jeff was stalling, still on his knees, next to the dump truck. "You can take the teddy bear," Amy said, "but you can't take the truck. No, you can't take the Smurf ball, Jeff, you know that. You can leave it here for when you come back. One toy for each of you. It doesn't matter which, Lindsey. I don't care. I don't care! Choose one of the coloring books — take any book you want. Just bring it and come. You'll pick the truck up later, Jeff. C'mon, we don't have all day. Grandpa's waiting. Let's get going. I mean *now* —"

Long Distance

MAXI is leaving as I come in. He's Border collie crossed with something spotted, I forget what, and exceptionally intelligent. Of course, he's highly trained. Soon as he sees me, he sits. Any other dog would be jumping or barking. But not Maxi — he sits and waits, turns melting eyes upon me. As always, I'm enchanted, I melt on cue, bowing at once to shake his paw and receive his trembling kisses. Only after we've had our greeting do I rise and properly greet his owner, Lil Robinson. As we begin to chat, Maxi's tail sweeps the linoleum, and I bend down to him again right in the middle of a sentence. Maxi is overjoyed by this. His hindquarters squirm — he can't contain his wag, his ID badge clatters against his other tags. The badge reads MAXI: PET THERAPIST — no kidding, that's what it says — while I'm merely CORA MILLER: HOSPICE VOLUNTEER. Lil is also only a volunteer.

The staff's apt to be more relaxed on Sundays, since the higher-ups in administration rarely show their faces. That's how it is today: the second floor deserted, and a pared-down crew on first — where the patients are. Patients and families:

it's family day, everything informal. Not that things ever get really formal around here — it's a question of degree. Dr. Danner's lounging around in chinos and a plaid shirt. He's come in without his stethoscope, and now he's rummaging around in the drawers of the desk at the nurses' station in search of one. He finds Sharon's, in a mess of other things, and yanks it out, raising it arm's length. Squints at it as though he can't quite recognize the thing. As if it might bite — a snake or something. The tubing is candy colored, the brightest of cherry reds.

"Why do they make these so *long?*" he asks, and answers himself, "It's ridiculous!" He fishes around in the drawer some more, dredges up a pair of scissors. Then he detaches the diaphragm, slicing off a good two inches of tubing from the midpiece, and reassembles it so neatly you'd never know he's touched it. Sharon, when she comes in tomorrow, may take a while to notice. When she does, she won't be pleased.

Then Dr. Danner starts off down the hall to make some visits, the nurses retreat to their conference room to work on their charts, and I set off, too, on my business — wheeling a cart of dirty linen down to the door marked BIOHAZARD. I check the disposal room early on in my shift as a rule; it's a way of getting my bearings.

There have been a bunch of baths — I can tell by all the toweling. And at least one death: I'm guessing from the egg-crate mattress left here. The table beside the sink is crowded with floral baskets of white plastic, the same braided handle on each, cut from the same mold. All the flowers are gone from them; only the filler greens remain, ferns, and dark, glossy leaves — real ones, but so shiny they too look plastic.

Two balloons drift overhead, both silvery, heart shaped, ribbons trailing. They're inscribed, I see. One says: FRIENDS FOREVER, the other: HOPE YOU'RE FEELING BETTER. Is it only

me — keeps running into all the messages everywhere, I wonder. So many messages . . . I knot the bag of dirty linen tight,
vaulting it into the bin. On my way out, I must be accidentally
brushing one of those dangling ribbons — it's FRIENDS FOR-
EVER — the balloon starts drifting after me, like it's leashed
and means to follow me out the door. I give it the back of my
hand, and it sails up and away again, settling close to the other
one.

Passing room 108, I sort of kneel — or keel — Mentally, I
mean, only in my head. From the outside, I trust, nothing shows,
maybe I slow a little, that's all. Someday I'll be able to pass by
untouched. But not yet. And today is turning out to be one of
the harder days. For some reason I'm jolted, stunned, as if for
the first time — the stab of memory sharp as it's ever been.

I spent hours sitting and waiting in that room, and in the alcove outside it, while my husband, Kenneth, slept and woke
and slept again. He died four years back. Sometimes it seems
like my whole life played out right here.

His last morning's still fresh in my mind. I see myself parting
the curtains, letting the daylight seep in. Kenneth's latest sleeping bout had gone on uninterrupted since the afternoon before — about fifteen hours, all told. Nothing I could do about
it, though I was desperate to rouse him. Then the light opened
on his face, and all of a sudden his lids lifted. He looked at
me — seemed to — and announced firmly and clearly: "We're
going to Spokane." Why Spokane? I didn't know what in the
world to make of it, but didn't have a chance to ask because,
no sooner said than he was back to sleeping again. Our oldest
daughter, Dot, had lived in Spokane briefly, after college, but
we'd never gone there to visit, and she'd moved away from
there years ago.

What he said bothered me quite a bit because Ken had

always been so precise on times and places, facts and reasons. Those weren't his final words, but they were the last he spoke in any language I recognized. The rest was all lost on me, impossible even to tell where one word ended or the next began. And I haven't yet figured out what he wanted us to do in Spokane. Had I been smart enough to know what to ask, or listened better, maybe . . .

I pass 108 again and again in the normal course of my rounds and, mostly, it's gotten easier, as time goes on. It really has. But every once in a while — like today — I'm nailed. I fight it, try to tell myself that my particular grief ought to be over and done with; seeing so many others come and go from that room should dilute things. But, too often, the very opposite happens: it's Kenneth's death *multiplied,* each new face only a new mask for the one face I miss the most. And there's that same old lurch of longing — *oh, Ken, how could you?* — the loneliness unabated, and the same old litany — *what I wouldn't give* —

I do and do not want this wound to heal. It's a connection, at least, the lines of communication still stretched, if throbbing. I must go on by, though, must drag myself on past; it's the den I'm headed for, three doors up ahead. I mean to give the Ramirez family a peek, see how they're faring. They've been camping out in the den for most of the week. I knock and enter.

And find them all still here. The family is huge; I only know a few of their names. Theirs is a hive-life, unimaginable to me as, I suppose, it is to most Anglos. The room is warm with bodies, abuzz with talk. Most of the sleeping bags and blankets are piled in a heap in front of the fireplace, but the younger kids are lounging on the remaining bedrolls, watching television, an ad for spicy corn chips. The chips, wearing sombreros and Spanish skirts, are leaping out of the bowl, shouting *"Olé!"* and clicking castanets for crispness.

The older folk have put two tables end to end to make one long one; they're sitting around it, picking at the remnants of a meal. They invite me to sit and have a bite with them, but I tell them that I've already eaten. I ask Mrs. Ramirez how her husband is doing. She shrugs — "*así así*" — spreading her hands wide. We have a very brief conversation, as much as my Spanish will bear.

The Ramirez family has gathered here from all over the Panhandle, from towns as distant as Texoma, Vega, and Sunray. I envy them in a way, marveling how strong families — mine is not — draw in at times like this. It's like the closing of an open wound, or the mending of a rip in a fabric, the threads drawing tighter around the tear, keeping the fabric whole.

As I step back out into the hall, I can hear one of the phones ringing at the nurses' station. Seems like nobody's picking it up, so I move towards it quick as I can, which turns out to be half a minute after Adele. "Mrs. Carver's in 113," I hear her say. While talking, she strokes the desk blotter with a ballpoint pen. It's leaving no mark, so she stabs it, making pockmarks in the blotter, then strokes again. No use: most of the pens here are dry. "You can dial the room directly," she says, though I'm shaking my head no. Has she forgotten? It can't be done. Then Adele covers the mouthpiece with her hand: "Would you run and pick it up over there, Cora?"

"Okay . . . ," I say, "*but* —" Mrs. Carver, the patient in 113, has had a stroke. She can't really speak anymore, not in English. Not in whole words of any kind.

Adele shrugs and covers the speaker end of the receiver with her hand. "It's long distance — her niece in California wants to talk to her. She can listen and understand even if she can't answer."

"Okay, then —" I'll do what I can. Here goes nothing, I think.

In 113, the phone is ringing away. Mrs. Carver is lying on her side, a pillow between her knees, resting. The cover's been thrown back. She's awake, one eye open wide, yet doesn't seem to notice the sound. I hurry the receiver over to her, lift it over the rail, press the earpiece to her ear. She sort of nestles, bunches up with her whole body, head, spine, knees curving round the instrument. Her hand comes up to touch the mouthpiece, so I pry her fingers open to make a holding cup. Once the thing seems secure, I let go, step back, wait.

I don't have to wait very long. She listens without speaking for maybe forty seconds, then begins her tirade, her long complaint, in that terrible mumble-jumble of hers. Her voice is harsh, still hoarse from all her shouting yesterday. I can't make out a syllable of what she's saying. It's all breakage — shreds, crumbles, I don't know what else to call it. And getting more rumbling the longer she keeps at it. Then quiet all of a sudden — she drops the phone.

Drops it, or throws it?

I'm stooping to pick it up, and I can hear the voice at the other end, tinny, small, but sharp: "Hello? Anybody there? Hello? Is this some sort of joke?"

"Hold it a second," I say. "The phone fell out of her hand. I'm going to give it to her again. Okay? Hold on."

"Hello — hello? Who *is* this?"

"My name's Cora. One of the volunteers. If you'd like to talk to somebody —" I mention the name of Mrs. Carver's regular day nurse and the name of her doctor if she wants answers to medical questions. Then I return the phone to the patient, adjusting the receiver as before. I mean to keep my hand under the mouthpiece now, but Mrs. Carver shoves it away. It's amazing how strong she still is. The same thing happens this time, only she sounds, if anything, louder, faster, angrier now. Once again, she drops the phone.

For a second time, I try to explain to the niece, who's sounding a bit blurry herself at this point. She's snuffling back tears (I can hear it) and speaks haltingly. "Should I try one more time?" I ask. "I can't promise the same thing won't happen. It probably will. I'll do my best, though —" It's an empty promise. Just as well the niece doesn't take me up on it, because Mrs. Carver has now closed both eyes, her way — she did it often enough yesterday for me to recognize it — of shutting things out, making them go away.

"No, wait," the niece says, "you still there?"

"I'm right here."

"Do you know her at all?"

"A little," I say. As well as anybody here — which is next to nothing, if truth be told. I fed her yesterday, took her for a walk in the wheelchair, helped her on and off the commode. That's only since yesterday, when they brought her in. This is the first I've looked in on her today.

By now the niece is weeping quietly at the other end of the line. I'm standing, bedside, waiting in silence while she tries to collect herself.

"Look," I improvise, trying to project a confidence I scarcely feel. "I think she understands everything you say. I think so. She knows you called to say you care. But she can't say it back. She's trying — but she can't."

"Could *you* understand it? Any of it?"

"Some," I say. "When she's not too excited."

It's not really a lie. Yesterday I guessed a few words: "awa" was "water" and, once in a while, "I want"; "sta" was "stop"; "un" was "no." She clawed my hand for "yes," though she did the same for "stop" — so that's "yes" *and* "no." "Verly" is somebody's name. Female, I think. Somebody close. Vernie? Laverne? "Swee" was "sweet" — I'm guessing, leaping in my mind, no one to contradict me. Once I heard her say "beheh

nagg" and the meaning floated clear — "beg him not to go" —
it came to me by reading the situation. A young man, former
pupil or somehow related, had been visiting; he was reaching
for his jacket, fixing to leave. Once, when she was perfectly relaxed, she said "bells," soft and clear, the word fully shaped.
Complete. I don't know what prompted it. But that's all — I'm
still guessing — I can't be sure.

"You heard her talking to me now — could you make heads
or tails of it?" the niece asks. She's grasping at straws, as desperate as I'd be — as I've *been* — in her shoes.

I have to confess that I couldn't make out a word of their
conversation. "She was much too excited," I say.

"What's she doing now?"

"Sleeping, it looks like." I doubt it. I think it's too much for
her to handle, so she's faking sleep.

"Listen," the niece says, "I want you to know what she was
like, somebody's got to know. She used to sing — she has the
loveliest singing voice. I want you to know who she is . . ."

So I listen, notice how she's saying "was" and "is," all
scrambled together; I stand there, the wire stretched how many
hundreds of miles between us, bending my ear to a stranger's
voice as she tells me.

Tour

A MAN, and a half, coming together in the hall, that's what they looked like from a distance. The two Fathers nodded, and that was that. The tall one went on swiftly, moving under his own steam, powerful legs pumping past. The other — the half — halted, then started up again in his slower way, the power not his own.

The power now is Olive's. She'd halted Father Arkady's wheelchair and backed off momentarily, thinking that the two priests might want to talk shop or at least pass the time of day. But no, apparently not. Seeing her mistake, she tightened her grip on the handle of the wheelchair and started to push again. No love lost between those two, that much was clear. Not a word, not so much as a lifted hand or a backward glance passed between them. Father Martin was, as usual, busy-busy, running to keep up with his beeper. All the same . . . a little courtesy costs nothing, Olive thinks, and she blames Father Martin. Father Arkady was hospice chaplain from back in the days when the place first opened; Father Martin, who followed, is still pretty much a newcomer, at it little more than a year. Now Father Arkady is a patient himself — his turn.

Olive has no particular use for priests or for preachers of any stripe, but when she went into Father Arkady's room to fetch him, she couldn't help noticing the touches he'd added here and there, trying to make the room a home. She didn't know what it was, exactly: maybe the plaster saint, with the chipped foot, and bird where a hand should be, that kept getting in the way of things on the sink, or that family portrait in an un-glassed frame — all those brothers and sisters ranged like fence posts in a long row. The meagerness of his possessions struck her. His priest robes hanging in the closet would have im-pressed her even if no one had told her they were to be his bur-ial clothes. The white robe and cape and the long scarf with its white embroidery, now yellowed with age, looked bridal al-most, but Father Arkady was never married. She feels the old man deserves something more at the end.

Olive steers Father Arkady round the bend and through the chapel door, away from the stained glass windows — they're far too bright this time of day. She presses forward, aiming for the gray space up front. This will do: the light's bound to shift; but, for the time being, his back is to the glare. She lines him up with the first pew, close enough to the altar for a good view of it, yet safely beyond touching distance so he won't be tempted to haul himself up to stand or kneel before it. That's a real dan-ger in his case. He can still stand, shakily — for all of a minute; kneeling is out of the question. From the little Olive has ob-served on her own, what the Romans do in their churches is surprisingly energetic in a stiff sort of way, and Father Arkady has a habit of overestimating his strength. He's so frail he can scarcely lift his arms unassisted. Olive recalls how he trembled with effort as the nurse helped him draw his clenched fingers through the armholes of his cardigan; she fears he may have exhausted himself beforehand in the struggle of getting dressed for this. You've only to glance at him to know what's what: his skin so pale, and near-transparent. The nurses have warned him about overtiring, though; as hospice housekeeper, simply lending an extra hand where needed, it's not Olive's place to add to what the nurses have told him.

When she stoops to make sure the brake on the wheelchair is set, Father Arkady cries out, "I can manage!" — his voice fierce, his hand skidding past Olive's, meaning to swat it away. Olive is stunned to see his lashes threaded with tears. Of course, he can't manage — they both know it. She reminds him that she'll be looking in on him every fifteen minutes or so. Then she shuts the door quietly behind her and leaves him to his business.

I can manage. . . . Soon as Olive's turned to go, Father Arkady begins to collect himself. He makes a reverence in the direction of the sanctuary, a bow of middling profundity from shoulders and neck, then blesses himself.

He's done his best to dress for this — civvies, but a clean sport shirt, pressed pants, his white-socked, swollen, feet stuffed into backless slippers. Not that it matters what he wears — pajamas, hospital gown, nothing at all — what difference could it make? He could pray in his room equally well, but coming round to the chapel to make his litany of remembrance at day's end is his old custom and, at his age, habits are not easily broken.

So little time! So much praying to get done. This is the only usefulness left to him now. Father Arkady glances at the altar. It's too high above eye level to examine the name cards or to count the long-stemmed roses, a full week's harvest, strewn across it. He'll do what he can to cover the lot in his general intentions — he has enough of a list, as it is. Best to start off in

the usual way with family and friends, then move on, parish by
parish, from Loome to Pep, Slade to Slocum to Prosper. Then
on to hospice. So many gone . . . Last week, with the help of
his address book, he'd taken a written census of those he ought
to pray for, and tallied a hundred and seventy-two names, with
a mere fifty-six left in the land of the living.

More now on the other side than this?

Not true. It's only that the names of the living keep on ac-
creting with marriages and births, the same and not the same.
Names and faces blur. He can't help thinking of last April,
when he made that visit to St. Joe's in Pep after — what? ten
years? Nine. . . . He hadn't been back since the parish had
that celebration for the burning of the mortgage papers, finally
all paid up, in '87. In the interval, everything — including
the placement of the tabernacle — had changed. Yet people
thronged him: "You remember Kennie, Father? You gave him
instruction the year before you left. . . ." Father Arkady said:
"My, how the children grow!" "You married us years ago, Father, remember us?" He said: "I remember your faces, but
you've got to help me out with the name." A woman, no longer
young, tapped him on the shoulder. "You were there when it
counted, Father, you listened when nobody else would. I wonder if you knew what that meant to me?" He hadn't known.
The woman's voice, low but insistent, was vaguely familiar to
him. *Almost* familiar. . . . What was it they'd talked about?
She didn't bring it up; he had no idea. And he'd brushed the
tribute aside, saying: "Everybody's been too kind."

So much he hadn't realized, hadn't given a second thought
to, but he was full to bursting on hearing these things and, even
today, simply recalling it makes him perk up in his chair, taller
by inches.

But enough of this basking! If he really intends to pray, Father Arkady reminds himself, he'd better quit rambling and get on with it. Start the way he usually does. With Rosa Arkady, his mother, for the repose of her soul . . .

What could it be *now?*

The walls, unfortunately, are thin. He can't ignore the mounting commotion in the entranceway, the scrape of voices and feet. Must be a tour setting out, one of the second-floor staffers leading it. He recognizes her voice, conjuring up a florid, puff-cheeked face, but not the name to go with it. Starting with *G*, wasn't it? Gla? Ga? Gladys? Gloria? Grace? He knew it once. . . . But why should it matter? What's important is — he hasn't forgotten the route or the script, and it's been years and years since he's led a tour. Seems strange to think back on himself as he was then, how smoothly the words flowed from his lips. Such a faint ripple of feeling. . . . Too little feeling.

When Father Arkady tries to picture his own last hour, he thinks of the final flutter of breath high in the throat, his throat still full of names unspoken. Aside from that — only the warmth of holy oil and the words of absolution come to mind. He stands at the same fixed distance, next to, neighbor to himself on that final bed, staring and straining. And sees his own face in profile, in iron mask. A visitor, a perfect stranger, would see as much. Only two things he asks. First, not to be taken unaware. Then, not to die clutching and clinging. Surely his courage won't fail him at the end. Hasn't his whole life been in training for this time? He thinks sadly of Father Menotti at his death hour, clasping his tiny statue of the Blessed Virgin with such tightly clenched fingers it prompted one of the aides to whisper that the priest's struggle with Satan had begun. *Please, Lord, not that —*

No mistake — the voices are closer. Father Arkady has

become all ears. *Pray! Pray!* — he urges himself on, his mouth set in a thin, grim line.

Right then, he hears the word "chapel," the creep of hands on wood, and — dreadful! — the door parts, heads angling and jostling in the breach. Father Arkady turns and glares. "Oh . . . sorry . . . in use," the tour leader blurts. Not a bit sorry — she pries the door even wider, but mercifully stands arms extended, barring entry: "Explain in a sec. So sorry" — she speaks in both directions — to the group and to the solitary figure within. Father Arkady averts his face. Light streams through the stained windows at his back. Pointing to the rose panel, gesturing past Father Arkady's illumined ear, the tour leader's fingers are dipped in the same crimson. She stage-whispers, "Everybody had a peek?" Father Arkady presents the back of his head to the crowd: *here's your exhibit.* He hopes his aggravation shows.

More whispering, murmurs. Then, gently, the doors fold shut. *Gone — good . . .* Father Arkady fairly weeps with relief.

Alone again, Father Arkady peers back over his shoulder to the window's blaze. He squints at the rainbow linking the panels; he knows by heart the text that goes with it. Said it himself, many a time.

Father Arkady is still listening as the tour group pauses in the hallway only a few steps away from the chapel door. The leader explains the theme of the stained glass windows they have not properly seen. She proceeds carefully from panel to panel: the rose, the tree, the crown of thorns, the cross, the butterfly, although it's all written out in the brochure. She halts at the mention of the rainbow to ask: "Anybody know what it means?" Then one of them answers, "Noah, isn't it? The rainbow after the flood?" followed by murmurs of recognition all around. One voice fattens on another. And the leader caps them all, intoning the words as scripted: "God's promise never fails."

"I knew it!" somebody murmurs. "I just knew it!" At last they are ready to move on, to enter the unit.

All gone.

Where was he? Intending to pray. In the pose of prayer. Pointed in that direction, barely started. Still, what did he expect — a power surge? Not likely. But freedom from distraction didn't seem too much to ask. And should be possible now. If only his belt weren't biting! It makes no sense that it should; he's no longer eating, yet his waist continues to swell. Protruding belly and peeking ribs — his body is stranger than ever to him. No help for it but to loosen the buckle a notch — no, make it two.

Now then. Father Arkady always closes his eyes to say his private prayers. The problem is: you never know what might pop into view. . . . Like Father Martin, now! Father Arkady is invaded by an image of the man's fleeting back, his legs working like pistons. Man like that ought to be coaching youngsters in sports — track, maybe. Far too energetic for hospice. So much energy makes sick people tired. Nothing Father Arkady can do about it, though; it's no longer his business. And it's trifling with God's time to dwell on it. *Let go* — he's got to.

He *means* to be praying. If he gets right down to it this very minute, he has enough time for little more than a bare roll call of names. And so he must. Right this minute.

Father Arkady starts over with his father, praying for the healing of memory, the repose of his soul. Then he moves on to his sister Vera. But here, his mind fidgets — he falters. The words will not go forward. So hard to imagine Vera healed or ever in repose . . .

*   *   *

Now they have passed the den and entered the patient care area. There are seven in the group — not counting the tour leader — two families and an unaccompanied young man. The leader, Ginny Madden, is keeping a watchful eye on the young man; she's been informed that he's casing the place for his wife, who can no longer be cared for at home. Standing outside the circle, he tends to stare at things Ginny's not pointing out. She hasn't seen him smile even faintly, even once. When they enter one of the empty single rooms, the others aren't afraid to press the mattress to assess its firmness, but he keeps his hands to himself; he's holding the hospice brochure coiled like a diploma in his right hand. He seems to be off in his own world, only half-listening. Ginny cants the bed up and down, showing off the electronic controls. She plays with the dimmer switches, extolling the light over the bed, light that need never be harsh.

Then Ginny points out the view from the window, and the wide door through which the bed can be wheeled into the open air of the courtyard. "And not only the bed!" she adds, launching at once into her horse story. The story never fails: the lonely cowpuncher languishing in bed, hankering for his horse, Lucky, companion of so many roundups, how the other cowpunchers brought Lucky in for a visit, leading the horse through one of these wide, bed-accommodating courtyard doors, clup-clupping all the way, right to the patient's bedside, and how man and horse were able to nuzzle a bit and have themselves a proper farewell. Ginny isn't making the story up; the tale is true, although it happened only the one time. The tale works like a charm, though, every time. Like now: nearly everyone who hears it can't help smiling.

And now the tour group is following Ginny out through the wide door into the courtyard, turning to note the benches, the bird feeders, the picnic tables and barbecue grills. One of the group comments, "Sure is pretty!" They all gaze up at the sky, so blue today, and breathe deeply of the unconfined air.

Next, it's on down the hall to the bathing room. "This is one of the favorite rooms of our patients," Ginny begins. "Many of our patients haven't been able to take a tub bath in weeks or months. Sometimes in years." She describes the large blue cart on wheels, now out of sight, occupied in one of the patient's rooms, explains how it is fitted to the bed, the patient shifted onto it. How the patient is covered for transit, then uncovered, lowered into the whirlpool, still supported by the cart, and the entire tub raised to save the nurses from straining their backs. "It's all hydraulics, a wonderful thing. . . . And while we're on the subject of wonderful things" — she recounts the tale of a baptism performed in the tub. "Last bit of unfinished business. . . . Died peacefully minutes later. He was not yet quite dry. The pastor came out of this room, his face glowing." This is another tale that never fails, and it, too, happens to be true. The group receives it, murmurs, smiles, affirms it. Only the young man standing slightly apart shows no expression. Steady attention is all, like a beam of a very white light.

As they step through the door, Ginny spies the blue bath cart, heading towards them from the end of the hall, and quickly herds the members of her group in the direction of the family room. They follow rapidly as she beckons. The cart is laden, the patient on it — motionless, swaddled in blankets from head to foot. Looks like a boat, with the nurse at the prow walking backwards and the other nurse steering from the stern. Only one member of the tour group has failed to make way for the approaching cart: it's the expressionless young man, who's staring at the patient as if to engage him in a conversation or force an answer to an urgent question. The patient's eyes are open, but he looks neither to the right nor to the left; his stare is fastened on the ceiling, as if to a rail. The cart swerves past the bystander and disappears into the bathing room. No contact is made. Ginny hails from down the hall: "Over here . . . the family room." But the young man gives no sign of hearing her. He stares at the door of the bathing room now closing. Stands there, unmoving. Then drops the brochure and fumbles to retrieve it, trying not to let his fingertips graze the floor.

Where was he? Who's he leaving out? If he'd brought his rosary along, Father Arkady might have been able to concentrate better. But so simple an act as holding the beads has become tricky lately, his hands given to inexplicable quakings, rippling spasms of thumb and forefinger. Anyway, it's only natural, reciting a bunch of bare names, that one of them sets him adrift along some tangent or other. Could happen to anyone at any age. And what's the point of all these lists? As if God needs reminding! It's praying with his hands held tight to his chest, what it amounts to. Trouble is — the minute he lets up on the lists, dreaminess takes over, past and future, here and elsewhere, all equally present. And when he thinks of his funeral in Prosper, as he so often does these days, it's as if he's actually there, as real as anything. He can pick out the spot where he'd want to be sitting — fourth pew from the back, center aisle, where the procession starts. Here the coffin will be met and blessed.

He's come early to avoid crowding. Warily, he regards the unpadded plank of the kneeler, so unfriendly to aged knees. But he's forgetting — hardness is no longer a consideration. The church is near empty, only ushers and choir members bustling importantly about. One of the lectors is practicing the reading from Isaiah: "*He will destroy on this mountain the covering that is cast over all people, the veil that is spread over all the nations . . ."* "*All* people," he tries again, shading it differently, "*all* the nations." No one seems to find it strange — or even to notice — that Father Arkady's sitting here, listening in.

Someone new to him is directing the choir. Sounds like it's happening top of his head, he can't miss a word of her scolding. She's reminding them that the bishop and the priests from all over the diocese are coming today, and don't they want to impress their visitors? No, she amends that — *impress* is the wrong word — don't they want to show what a deep, strong faith they have here at St. Joe's?

No mention of Father Arkady, whose occasion this is.

They run through the psalm, the communion song, the song of farewell. "Can you make that special *oh* sound? That most beautiful sound? Remember how the mouth goes? *Yes,* the same note." It's always been this way: some of the singers don't read music. "*Of course,* it sounds the same every time. Of course!" They start afresh on the Te Deum, but are no sooner begun than the choir leader breaks it off again. "You're singing in your talking voices. Talking isn't singing — *Sing!*"

They resume. Then a tremendous rumbling from the pedal bass drowns out everything.

The young man who strayed has returned to the fold. The other members of the tour group close ranks, following Ginny from corner to corner of the family room. They observe, without speaking of it, the spillover from somebody's all-night vigil, sleep clothes and blankets crumpled on the couch. Ginny points out the working fireplace, the dining table, now littered with bags of chips and grimy paper plates, tells them how the room can be reserved for birthdays, anniversaries, and such. The group crowds briefly into the narrow kitchen to view the electric stove, microwave, refrigerator with ice maker — there's an outside chute, you don't even have to open the door.

They pass the nurses' station and the supply room. At the Tremain Suite, a showplace, they — all but the one — step inside to sample the quiet. Everything is muted here: the soft couches and wing chairs covered in fabrics of pastel and rose. "No windows, so it's a good place to catch up on sleep," Ginny points out. "And," sounding almost like an afterthought, "it's the most private room on the floor, so families often gather here after a death. . . . Any questions?" There are no questions. The young man remains standing on the threshold; he holds the brochure by its corner now, as if it's been soiled by its fall.

The tour is winding down.

The place prepared for him isn't far off. Farther Arkady's procession follows the coffin out the door, down the winding, unpaved path, into the chuchyard. The priest-pallbearers and Father Arkady's few surviving kin lead the double file: his nephew Al, two grandnieces who've made it down from Missouri. Sophie, his last surviving sister, herself ailing, is absent. Not so many of his generation left now, but his other family, just as real, is all around him — the Rossiters and Galans, Hoelschers, Dettons. His best memories are here at St. Joe's. Closest thing to home.

His casket is topped with a single spray of flowers — roses and lilies mixed with wildflowers. He never wanted the fancy hothouse flowers, they're too humid, heavy — but they're not the important part. It's the place — he's relieved — *his* place, the spot they'd promised him, it's waiting. Looming above him: Our Lady of the Fields, standing waist deep in wheat. Barberry hedge, cottonwoods and cedars, and the stones of his friends extend in widening semicircles around him. It takes a few minutes for the procession to wind its way and cluster around the bishop, whose steepled miter can be seen from a long way off. It's a quiet scene: the mourners sidestepping — look like they're wading — trying not to trample the graves, the bishop intoning, starting to drone and — isn't that Jake Wilhelm's son? That's Buddy — isn't it? — waiting on the other side of the hedge, leaning on his backhoe and staring at his dust-scuffed boot, amazed at how deep the dryness goes, parched all the way, six feet down.

They certainly do need rain. The wheat won't be worth harvesting without it, the milo not worth planting. Here and there, a parishioner glances up, over the church steeple, searching for any hint of cloud. But the sky is clear and crystalline, vacant; the light dazzles, heartlessly bright.

Three times the bishop raises his arm with a scything motion, bringing it down in a gust of holy water. Father Arkady is asperged for the last time, each of the priests dipping and casting in turn. Each has his own way: Father McSherry — tremulous; Father Martin — crisply efficient; Father Holman, Father Grooms, and those who come after, repeating the blessing with brisker, ever more abbreviated strokes. It is done. Slowly, the air fills with sound: intermittent birds, leaf chat, the cough of an old motor, straining to turn over. Faces turn: to the parking lot and the street, and the other stones. The crowd begins to seep away.

Now the great forsaking begins.

What's for lunch? There's a wonderful spread at the parish hall — three kinds of pie! With them, Father Arkady cannot go. The clamps seem to tighten now, he is robed in lead. Human voices, faces, fade; not one angel in view. The angels of stone scattered among the crosses, the tablets of stone, don't count; nothing descends or takes to the air. Only a bird drilling the fresh-turned soil, edge of the pit. Sounds like a question it's piping — *"keep? keep?"*

Olive has come by, peeking in on Father Arkady, and gone silently on her way. He looked all right to her, though bowed, wound down into himself, staring at his lap with the concentration of somebody piecing a watch together. Praying, she guesses, really into it.

From his far place, Father Arkady hears the door open and softly shut. He stares at his feet, at the green shadows cast by the light in its westward passage, now drifting through the panel with the great tree emblazoned. The trees so much smaller where he's at . . .

They're cottonwoods, shuddering in the breeze, leaves streaming. Sound like water. In air dry as bone. Everyone's gone now. All but one — a woman whose face is so downcast as to be veiled from him. Someone unsure of her place, having to wait until all the others leave.

Who is she? Living or dead? Has he prayed for her yet? She draws closer; stands, head bowed, at his side. Who could she be? Her lips move — if only she'd speak up! — but no speech comes through except for the whisper of hands, of her hands palming the flank of the casket, caressing the wood. Then, abruptly, the hands lunge for a rose deep in the heart of the spray, seize —

The bundle breaks — the blooms scatter —

When she touches the rose to her cheek, Father Arkady almost feels it, first the sharp tug, then the faint coolness against his own cheek — cool and slow — the texture of breath. The ghost of a texture. Then the woman turns to leave.

"Oh, wait —"

She halts, raises her head. And now he sees: it's Vera. Who else *could* it be?

"I'm so glad you've come," he says, "you've no idea."

The last time he saw Vera among the living was right before her release from the hospital. An unauthorized release: Father Arkady had pushed for it because he knew she wouldn't give him a moment's peace unless he consented. Vera had been, as usual, depressed and taking things: alcohol, uppers, downers, whatever she could get her hands on. "She'll *use*, you know," the doctor had warned him. "I'm writing down *AMA* — that's 'against medical advice.'" And then he'd muttered something under his breath, something that sounded like "She goes to her destruction." Father Arkady had scarcely registered the last remark at the time, but he'd never forgotten it. He didn't know whether the doctor actually said "destruction," or whether he — Father Arkady — only thought this to himself. He'd never be sure. What he did know was: that moment of consent marked the exact point where he'd finally given up on Vera — handed her over to herself and been relieved of her. *Felt* relieved — immense, shameful, undeniable relief. She'd worn him down at last. He had Confirmation that weekend, too, parents — there were other people in the world! — and, on top of that, the bishop was coming, staying overnight; he couldn't have Vera ringing up the rectory every hour, as she was sure to do if held against her will. As it turned out, she hadn't overdosed on that particular weekend but weeks later — another hospitalization, another release. Even so.

"I need," Father Arkady begins. Halts. When he speaks again, his voice is very low — "your blessing."

"My what? *Me*? Bless?" Vera gives one of her soft laughs. "Ego, Aram — it's always been your game. Thought you could save me and you failed. Still think you can save the world?"

"I'm so sorry —"

"Ego, Aram, I'm telling you. You were always my favorite in the family, but there was nothing anybody could do to stop me — not even you."

"I *need* your forgiveness —"

"Oh well, then — given." She shrugs, humoring him perhaps, and then, in a slow wave, voice and image fading, "Can't . . . stay . . ."

Olive finds Father Arkady still praying, the air around him watery green, tinged with blue; it's downright creepy. Much too quiet. The old man is hunched over; only the crests of his shoulders move — he's still breathing, at least.

But then, suddenly, he turns to greet her. Speaks: "Thought I'd lost you." Olive isn't at all sure the remark is meant for her. They meet, in this strange light, shadow to shadow. Olive can't really make out his face, the features or expression, only the tilt of it, how it's lifted, set for the first time full upon her. And, though she's certain his chair hasn't moved an inch since she parked it the hour before, she could swear he's traveled.

The Juniper Tree

I HAD TO AGREE to the mother's terms before she would allow me to sit with her daughter while she was away. I must, on no account, let on to the child how sick she was. "We try not to say the D-word around her," is how she put it. Although the child was nowhere within earshot, the mother said this in a very small voice. "Of course, sometimes it's unavoidable," she added, "but you understand what I'm trying to say — we never apply the word to *her*. It's for her own protection."

The child's name was Marian. She was the frailest of eight-year-olds. Her emaciation was extreme: I'd heard she'd been living on crushed ice, mainly, with sometimes a spoonful of sherbet or cake. Even her mother had given up insisting that she eat more. Her face was still puffy from one of the steroids they'd tried and given up on; her pale hair was patchy, scant.

She'd been sitting up in bed, hunched over the bed table, when I came in. A bed much too big for her, I might add. There was a cup with ice water and a plate with a cube of white cake, shoved way to the side of the table to make room for her papers — some sort of list she was copying, printing in block letters, painstaking line by line. I noticed then how bruised her arms were, and that she was surrounded by lamb's wool. I'd been instructed not to hug or touch her at all, unless she expressly invited me to. Even the lightest touch could be painful for her. "My skin blues easy," she said without seeming to glance up. I guess I must have been staring.

I was sent in to distract Marian when her mother — who more or less lived at hospice, sleeping in Marian's room, cooking in the family room, doing her laundry here — had to to be elsewhere. Some ceremony at her older daughter's school, not a graduation — an honors assembly, I think. I'm not sure. Important, anyway, or she wouldn't have considered leaving Marian's side. Before I stepped into the child's room, I'd gathered up what I could in the way of books and toys. I had no idea at what level she was capable of reading, since she'd been ill — and, I assumed, out of school — for so long. Three out of eight years is long.

I'd come in with an armful: coloring book and crayons, a jigsaw puzzle — one of the easier ones, I forget how many pieces, a Monopoly set, a Dr. Seuss book I imagined she could read on her own, and a book of fairy tales in small print I could read aloud to her if she wanted.

I made the mistake of spreading out the array at the end of the bed. She showed no sign of interest, scarcely lifting her eyes from what she was copying, and then only to glance at the clock. When I pushed forward one item after another, asking her which one she'd like to do after she was done with her writing, she made it very clear that my visit had not been *her* idea. "You shouldn't of bothered," she said. "My mom's coming back in less than an hour. I've got a lot of work to do before then — I can't waste time." I knew that her mother couldn't possibly be back in less than two or three hours, and felt certain her mother had told her as much, but I saw no point in contradicting Marian right at the start.

She was busy keeping up with her schoolwork, it seemed. I don't know whether the school was sending over regular assignments, or whether a classmate brought them in from time to time, or a tutor for the homebound, or what the arrangement was. It could have been that Marian was reviewing old material — it hardly mattered one way or the other. The list she was copying out was spelling and vocabulary; she was "doing English." It was her "most favorite subject," as she would confide to me later.

Rebuked, I settled on the sofa and silently leafed through the titles and illustrations in the fairy-tale book. I was waiting for my cue to redeem myself and become useful. It was a while coming. Marian worked away doggedly, only glancing up every ten minutes or so to stare at the clock. My patience paid off, though, for at last she turned to me and asked about *c-h-a-n-n-e-l*. She recognized the word from television, but had no idea, until I told her, that there were other meanings. I expressed an interest in seeing the rest of the list when she was done, and offered to give her a practice quiz on it. To my surprise, she eagerly agreed to this. "But when I'm ready," she said. "I'm not ready yet." Then she asked, "What do you do in your real life?"

"Isn't this real life?" I asked.

"You know — before you came here. Were you a teacher?"

I had to admit that I'd always loved school but never had become a teacher like I'd planned. Instead I'd gotten married and raised kids. But I'd given my kids practice quizzes before they took their exams, and they usually did well — not always, but usually.

This was the list: *eagle, smell, all, seagull, glistened,*

gleaming, channel, full, single, little, screeching. On the back of the page, Marian had used five of the spelling words in sentences: *All my toys are in the room. The seagull smells like fish. I am little. I made a channel. It's gleaming.*

She'd misspelled only *glistened,* putting in an *a* for the first *e.* I complimented her on her sentences, giving her an A plus on them. She asked if I was very old. "Old enough," I said.

"Old enough for what?" she asked.

"Oh, it's just an expression. That's what people say when they don't want to tell their age — women mostly, who don't like having wrinkles. It's silly. I'll be going on sixty."

"My mom's going to Becka's graduation in June," she announced. Again, she monitored the clock — it was a bit unnerving. "Becka's going to high school next year."

"That's nice," I said. Dumb comment, but I couldn't think of anything better to say. "For them," she added.

Then she confided, "I'm not getting any more shots. No more drips. No needles."

"That's good," I said, knowing that it wasn't, knowing that she knew it wasn't. She was testing *me* now, and I was failing.

She was a very bright child, wise beyond her years, and brimming with curiosity. When she asked me my name, I said she could call me Cora, that everybody here did. This wouldn't be allowed, she reminded me, if we were in school now, if I were her teacher. She went on to ask about my husband and his work, then more about my children — their names and ages, what they were doing now they were grown, whether I missed them. Then back to my husband: "Why did he die?" I told her the name of his disease. "Does it hurt very much to die?"

I said I didn't think so, and cast about in my mind for a rapid change of subject. But then, abruptly, she did the changing for me, or, at least, that's what I thought she was doing at first. In fact, she was far too quick for me. She asked, "What are mayflies, anyhow?"

She had me there. "Can't say I've ever seen one," I answered. "Or read about them. Why? They're not on your vocabulary list. Why do you want to know?"

"How long do they live?"

Oh. I could see all too clearly now where she was heading. I shrugged.

"Two hours? Three? A week? A day?" she pressed. "Can't you tell me?"

"Oh, gosh, I don't know that either," I answered truthfully. "Not very long, I guess."

"But not-very-long is long for them, isn't it? It's a whole lifetime — for them."

"I guess it must be."

"That's what I thought. . . ." She sighed, and asked me to lower the head of the bed, "but only a teeny bit." I scooted the table away, over to the side, while I was at it. I figured she'd worked long enough.

"How about some reading?"

"I'm pooped," she said. "Anyway, my mom's coming back in a few minutes. Why isn't she back already?"

"I'll read to you."

"I can read to *myself,*" she said scornfully.

I assured her that I knew that, but sometimes it was nice to be read to. How about if *she* picked out the story? I decided Dr. Seuss was out of the question; it was way too young for her. I handed her the book of fairy tales, propping it up on a pillow I placed on her stomach in case it proved too heavy for her to hold.

The book was called *Children's All-Time Favorite Fairy Tales.* I didn't know enough to wonder at the title at the time.

Leafing through it, she picked out "The Juniper Tree" because she noticed at once, just by scanning, that the girl in the story had a name almost like her own: Ann Marie was a lot like Marian, with the two names stuck together backwards. It seemed a good enough reason for choosing the story, and I began reading.

By the time I realized what a dreadful story it was, it was too late. Either I'd never read "The Juniper Tree" before or I'd completely forgotten it. The problem was that it all began so innocently, with a childless woman's wish to have a child, the passage of seasons from winter to spring to summer, and, in due course, the birth of the child of her wish. How could I have known what was coming?

A month went by, the snow was gone; and two months, and everything was green; and three months, and the flowers came up out of the ground; and four months, and all the trees in the woods sprouted and the green branches grew dense and tangled with one another and the little birds sang so that the woods echoed, and the blossoms fell from the trees; and so five months were gone, and she stood under the juniper tree and it smelled so sweet her heart leaped and she fell on her knees and was beside herself with happiness; and when six months had gone by, the fruit grew round and heavy and she was very still; and she snatched the juniper berries and ate them so greedily she became sad and ill, and so the eighth month went by, and she called her husband and cried and said, "When I die, bury me under the juniper . . ."

When it came to the part about the child of her wish being born and the mother feeling "so happy that she died" — that was a bit much, "the D-word," but not only that, a most peculiar reason for dying — a warning beeper should have gone off in my mind. But the first child, the child of the wish made under the juniper tree, was a boy; we still hadn't gotten to the part where Ann Marie came in, and I didn't think it was fair to stop short of that. That was with the husband's second marriage, a second child, this time a girl. Then the second wife — the stepmother of the boy — began showing her true colors. She loved her own daughter, Ann Marie, but she hated her stepson and took to pushing and pinching him. The wicked stepmother was a pretty standard fixture of fairy tales, and I noticed how fully the story held Marian's attention — she hadn't glanced up at the clock once in all this long preface, so I read on heedless of what lay ahead.

It's when I came to the boy's beheading — the part about the stepmother's opening a trunk and inviting the boy to pick out one of the prize apples inside it, and then, when he leaned in to see better, slamming the lid down on him, so that his head was sliced off and tumbled among the apples — that I should have had enough sense to pause a minute and scan the story remaining. If not there, then immediately afterwards, when the stepmother stuck the boy's head back on, tying a handkerchief around his neck to hide where it was cut through, then setting him on a chair by the door with an apple in his lap, to look as though he were still alive. And when Ann Marie knocked his head off again because he would not give her his apple, there, at least, I should have quit once and for all. But Marian was smiling quite cheerfully through all of this, and still hadn't glanced at the clock. And when I hesitated before turning a page, she said "Go on!" so eagerly that I didn't want to disappoint her, and I thought, too, it *has* to get better after this, and so I did read on.

Well! I was mistaken again. Things went rapidly from bad to disastrous. When I came to the part where the boy was chopped into gobbets of meat by his stepmother and the meat tossed into a steaming pot, where it was salted with Ann Marie's tears and stewed to perfection, I couldn't see how things could get any worse. I did slow down, in hopes of seeing my way a line or two ahead, but Marian noticed my change of pace, and again urged me on, saying: "Go on!" And this time she added, "I like this story. I know it's only a story." I reflected that this story might even be a relief for her. After all, Marian had already met her demons — real ones. And, besides, I said to myself, kids nowadays grow up with guns and gore all around them, not to mention ultrarealistic television and movie violence — and this story is quite amateurish, by today's standards. It's so clearly only pretend. And, besides, I thought: it would be worse to stop and leave off at this low point in the story than to move on ahead and see some things corrected, even though I couldn't, for the life of me, imagine how crimes like these could be corrected.

That was my thinking — why I blundered on. And when the father came home and ate all of the delicious stew, which had only just that morning been his own son, I felt for a certainty that we had scraped the absolute bottom, and that this time — it could not be otherwise — we were on our way up and out.

So I raced through the part where the story told how much the father enjoyed the stew, how he smacked his lips while he ate, and refused to share any of it with his family, devouring, all by himself, every last morsel to be had.

When Ann Marie went under the table to gather up all of her brother's bones, even the littlest, that her father had dropped there, to bind up the bones in her silk handkerchief, and lay the handkerchief on the ground in front of the juniper tree, Marian murmured approvingly, "I knew it!" And when the tree began to move its branches like someone clapping hands for joy, and the tree became mist, then fire, and a wonderful bird rushed upwards from the heart of the fire, and the handkerchief with the bones vanished without a trace, and the juniper tree became only a tree again, Marian murmured, "That's so neat. . . ." She spoke slowly, though, her head dipping, and I began to suspect she'd never hear it through.

But she roused herself once more, and said, "I think I'll try some cake." I moved the bed table back, and she broke off a morsel of cake with her fingers, placing it carefully on her tongue, and took a swallow of water to help make it go down. She did this twice, then asked, "What happened after that?"

Things got better only gradually, much too slowly for my purposes. The bird went from a goldsmith to a shoemaker to a miller, begging for gifts, singing a horrible song that somehow sounded beautiful to the people listening:

> *My mother she butchered me,*
> *My father he ate me,*
> *My sister, little Ann Marie,*
> *She gathered up the bones of me.*

I happened to glance over at Marian while I was chanting this, and was disappointed to find that her eyes were closed. I paused and tested her: no go. No more urging me to go on. Her eyes did not open. Her breathing was easy, though, she seemed to be sleeping soundly, a curve to her lips, as if she were enjoying a private joke. I didn't see how she could, but it really did look like smiling.

While she slept, I read on ahead silently and found out that, thanks to the goodness of Ann Marie and the juniper tree, everything really did turn out well in the end — except for the wicked stepmother, who — crushed by a millstone dropped from the bird's neck — got exactly what was coming to her. And how, out of the smoke and flame of the stepmother's destruction, the bird became a boy again, and the family complete. I hoped Marian would wake so we could see it through, but she was sleeping deeply by then.

When I was done reading the story to myself, I got up to stretch. I stood at the window, stared out. The trees in the courtyard were young, planted after the building was already in place. That would make them about as old as Marian, I thought. Tree time works on a different scale, of course. I thought I could name the different kinds they'd planted there — cottonwood, honey locust, Russian olive, pink lady, some kind of ash. . . . A straggling pear tree going from bloom to leaf. No juniper.

Marian's mother returned less than an hour later. Marian was still sleeping and, having no easily explained reason for remaining, I gathered up what I'd brought from the playroom, leaving mother and daughter alone together.

I have to admit I was terribly disappointed: I wanted to see the story through with Marian, to bring her through terrible evils to a righting of wrongs and a resolution. I wanted her to see it all spelled out, every detail accounted for. It was something *I* needed to do — I'm not sure it would have made a great deal of difference to Marian herself — she hadn't seemed in the least troubled by the goriest parts of the tale. I wondered whether she'd even remember our afternoon together when she awakened.

It's useless, though, going over and over this, since I never did get a chance to follow through.

I saw the child once more, a few days later. She was surrounded by her parents and one of the nurses, so I only caught a glimpse of her. She looked terribly pale. Really chalky —

even her lips. I asked if she wanted me to bring her any ice, a ridiculous question under the circumstances, but something, anyway, for me to do.

She raised her hand before speaking, like the good school-child she'd been, then breathed out "hurry!" — her voice barely a whisper.

I *did* hurry, fast as my legs would carry me. When I returned, not more than two, three minutes later, she seemed already half-disappeared, all but swallowed up by the sheets. I couldn't even make out her face, the top of her body was so hedged about by the backs of the adults tending her. The rest of her had curled into a fetal ball and, this time, no hand was raised.

Zone

WHEN HE FIRST came in last week, Mr. Straughn was still able to take a stroll down the corridor. He wore a bathrobe with vertical stripes, which accentuated his thinness. He was *terribly* thin: his ears jutted out, his jawline and Adam's apple had a chiseled clarity. And yet, with all this, he wasn't a bit stooped — still an imposingly tall figure, flanked by an equally tall wife and daughter, their long noses and determined chins so much alike they could have been taken for brother and sisters.

Nobody knew how much he was suffering, really. The consensus was that he was underreporting his pain because of the program he'd set for himself. He was mercilessly frank on some things, reserved or dissembling on others. His frankness was never impolite, but some of his other habits seemed out of character with it, like his insistence on calling me Mrs. Miller — never Cora — as I kept on asking him to do.

Slowly, one arm braced by his IV pole, the other supported by his wife, or sometimes his daughter, Mr. Straughn would make a complete circuit of all four corridors. On the return trip, he sometimes seemed on the verge of tottering, and he'd pause at the nurses' station to catch his breath, and to give us a piece of his mind. One of his favorite topics — or targets — was the glazed ceramic bowl on the desk, the one that's shaped like a basket. It's crudely made, all the joints showing; you can see how the clay was rolled, then braided and stacked in coils. A five-year-old could have shaped it as well. It wasn't the bowl that he was focused on, though, but what it contained: the prayer cards. "Counsels of confusion," he called them.

I, myself, have always had a problem with those prayer cards. They come out with perfectly opposite pronouncements on faith and death, and any other subjects they touch upon. One says to give over, let go, to enter before you know, another, coming right after it, to hold fast to what you already know; one says you find salvation by losing your way, another, that salvation is found only in "following Him." I, too, would like to see these contradictions resolved and laid to rest. Still, I ask myself, why can't all of it be true — *fall back, press on* — marking a sort of pulse, a tempo, with truth resembling a conversation or an argument, more than a monologue? I've never been strong on logic, though, and Mr. Straughn was, if nothing else, supremely logical. But I was starting to say — Mr. Straughn would lean against the desk there and fan through a handful of those prayer cards. He'd give a delighted hoot every time he spotted a contradiction, and he was still spunky enough to say: "Borrowed thoughts, secondhand language. I want to tell it fresh. I mean to. If it's at all humanly possible, I'll do it."

He meant to.

He was an agnostic and proud of it, sharp as a tack. Not an atheist, he insisted upon making the difference crystal clear. An atheist ruled things out in advance — he didn't. He neither believed nor disbelieved. As far as he was concerned, the evidence for or against there being a God could cut either way. The evidence "so far," he was careful to add. Mr. Straughn was open to possibility. As for what had already been written on the subject of dying, he'd read enough to have serious doubts about near-death experiences, all those enthusiastic accounts, so plentiful lately, of hovering over the hospital bed and one's body on the bed, free of the body and glad of it, or of moving through a dark tunnel towards an opening flooded with light, with long-departed grandparents cheering one on from the open end. We had our own small collection of such tales in the hospice library. The stories were much alike and always upbeat. They made you wonder why anyone ever bothered to linger in the land of the living.

"The big problem with all of that," Mr. Straughn objected, "is that none of those tale-tellers went over to stay. They're unreliable, because they didn't. You see what I'm saying. . . . Near-birth isn't born. Near-death isn't dead. None of them actually — I mean *finally*, irrevocably — died. They came back instead to write books and cash in their royalty checks. I'm going to cross over, no coming back, but I'll try to send messages as long as I can. Keep you informed. You understand what I'm saying?"

He should have been a teacher. "You understand what I'm saying?" was one of his favorite expressions. He wanted us to understand.

We all knew his plans. He wanted to record how it feels to die, what it meant to enter what he called the end zone, so that his wife and daughter, and we — all of us — would be better prepared for it. He had no tolerance for fantasy or "pious piffle." He expected us to stay tuned, to pay full attention. And there wasn't a single person on the staff, including Olive from housekeeping, who wasn't in on his plans and who hadn't been enlisted to help him when the time came. A few refused to come along, for personal religious reasons. But most of us, religious or not, were curious.

In my mind's eye, I could see my husband, my late husband, Kenneth, shaking his head over us, and smiling indulgently. How well I knew that smile . . . What it meant was: *all wrong!* Ken, too, was logical, a chemist by training, and long before his last illness, he'd given me his thoughts on death. Unlike Mr. Straughn, he had it all solved in advance. "I assure you, Cora, there's no problem" — I can hear him so clearly, that faintly irascible edge to his voice whenever he spoke in the name of reason — "no intellectual difficulty. It's the mind's own arrogance to think there is." So Ken's part was reason unmasking reason, I guess. The way he saw it, life and death were on a continuum; there were countless cell deaths going on before and after the brain quit. Ken liked to point to organ transplants: "How do you think eye banks and heart transplants work? Except for brain death, which nobody can get to the other side of and tell about, because you need the brain to be able to report with, there's no great dividing line to cross. And no mystery, Cora. Don't try to glorify it." That "no mystery" was aimed straight for what he liked to call my Catholic heart. For, however far I've strayed from the official Church, I never could gain the least foothold in Ken's unstoried world. And *my* world is still a place of intimations, and wonders, and unstoppable hope. Is this "Catholic," necessarily? But I'm straying again — it's Mr. Straughn's story I'm trying to tell —

Even Vinnie, our senior nurse, promised to do what she could to help him, despite her firm prediction that the project would never pan out. I think she was impressed by Mr. Straughn's consistency. Vinnie was a veteran; she'd been at hospice for eight years, and she had to admit that she'd never met anyone like him, so businesslike and calm. "If anyone *could* do what he intends to do — he's the man," she granted.

Of course we've all seen our share of controlling types, patients who demand to know on the hour what to expect next. Mr. Straughn was controlling, all right, but in a different way; he wanted to tell *us* firsthand what to expect, and reminded us continually to keep the channels of communication open. He instructed us to give him the nasal cannulae, never the full oxygen mask, no matter how hard he seemed to be struggling, so as not to muffle what he was trying to say. And I can't help saying this, though it sounds crazy: it was as if he were looking forward to what lay ahead, as if it were an opportunity that had opened up for him, a chance-in-a-lifetime research project.

He'd made his mark from his very first hour on the unit. "Could you rate the pain on a scale of one to ten?" Vinnie asked him. A perfectly routine question, read off from the admission form; she was expecting a routine answer. Mr. Straughn came right back at her with "five point two." Then paused for maybe half a second, and corrected himself: "Five point four would be more accurate." He was a watchmaker and a freelance inventor, used to precision. Five point four sounded like precision, but Vinnie's private opinion was that his pain was in the eight-to-nine range. Yet she had to take him at his word. It was obvious that he wanted the minimal pain medication because he was desperately afraid of any clouding of consciousness.

This Monday, when he entered what appeared to be a coma, I was called in to help Vinnie change his linens, which were drenched, and to draw him up in the bed. He roused himself, suddenly, as we were letting down the side rails. Came piping up with some sharp question about "gear ratios" — or "G-rays," it could have been — something neither of us could make head nor tail of, then he lapsed back into unconsciousness. Vinnie was so rattled she started to put the rubber glove on *his* hand instead of her own.

On Tuesday afternoon, he rallied. He seemed to be out of the woods, dozing more often, off and on, but still plenty alert in the waking intervals. He continued scribbling in his notebook much of the time, his wife pitter-pattering around the room, fetching and tending. He never again asked to leave the bed, though, and it seemed clear his walking days were over. But, of course, he had other work to occupy him.

By Thursday, Mr. Straughn was too weak to sit up or hold the pen, and he started in on the tape recorder. The daughter came and went — she had family of her own, but his wife was at his side day and night, taking whatever sleep she could on the sofa. She looked none too well herself. And she seemed to be as involved as her husband was with his project, helping him out by taking notes as backup. She didn't know shorthand, unfortunately, and could have used it, for sometimes, even then, he was too quick for her. So Mr. Straughn's daughter brought in a second tape recorder to ensure they wouldn't miss anything. It was one of those hand-held Dictaphone deals, not very practical because the tapes that fit it are so short-lived. Tapes, large and small, littered the bed, the bed table, even the sink. Seemed like Mr. Straughn was nearly always recording, although he dismissed all his observations so far as "practice — a preface" to the real thing. How did he say it? What he'd recorded so far was only a "sickbed journal," he wasn't yet in the "end zone." That's how he put it, perfectly matter-of-fact, looking over the playing field, so to speak.

He'd worked up yet another level of backup: an alphabet board for spelling the words, pointing them out letter by letter, in the event his voice gave out.

The day he'd been building towards came on Friday. As it turned out, it was a superbusy afternoon on the unit. Two admissions, one on top of the other. And the social worker had finally gotten Simon's father to visit his son. Simon is the seventeen-year-old with AIDS. His mother's been with him night and day, but his father, who separated when he learned about his son's illness, never once visited — until that afternoon. We all knew he was coming in and were prepared to be welcoming — and forgiving — "one small step for humanity," as Dr. Perry said. But, wouldn't you know it, that step was never taken, Simon's father never set foot in his son's room. Instead, he stood in the doorway and shouted in the direction of the bed: "You did it to yourself!" Simon started shaking so violently he had to be sedated after that. It would have been better had his father never tried.

It was a bad omen for promises kept, now that I think back on it, although Mr. Straughn's was a different case entirely — the human connection held to the end. That was the problem. His family simply wouldn't let him depart in lucidity and peace, despite the bargain they'd agreed to and reviewed daily. I don't know why things turned out the way they did. Their own fear, maybe. Or the need to give him comfort, reassurance, to smooth over suffering. Or just plain impatience — the urge to make things happen, rather than wait for them to declare their meanings. I'm not blaming anyone. But I am getting ahead of myself here —

That morning, Mr. Straughn had become officially "preactive"; by two-thirty, he was "active" — actively dying. We still didn't know how many hours or days the process might take. This was it, though, the crunch, what he'd been waiting for —

I made it my business to keep looking in. Any pretext: ice, which nobody wanted, lanolin for his dry lips, a damp washcloth to sponge off perspiration. There wasn't much sound in the room, except for the whirring of the tape recorders taking note of near-silence and the faint hissing of the building's ventilation system. Mr. Straughn was taking an oxygen assist — only the nasal cannulae; we'd kept to our promise of not using the mask, so as not to get in the way of his speaking. He was breathing higher and higher in his chest. He was also in some discomfort, if not outright pain, his neck rigid and hyperextended as the rest of his body began to slump.

His eyes were swimming in and out of focus, yet I think he saw me when I applied the washcloth. I took his cool hand and pressed it, and he said "zweh," for sweat, I guess. He tried to speak again when I came in to remove a lingering lunch tray, everything on it untouched. By then, his speech was whispered and seemed to be all vowels. I kept hanging out at the nurses' station, having used up all my excuses for entering the room, when the daughter paged me. "He wants witnesses," she explained. "I *think* that's what he said — I couldn't swear to it."

So I came in as a "witness" — one of those stiff standers by the bedside. There was the wife and the daughter, Olive from housekeeping, Louellen the LVN, and myself.

No question — Mr. Straughn was in the end zone, very close to what he was so curious to behold and reveal to us, each syllable of breath an effort. He was moving restlessly, incoherently, and at one point managed to throw off his sheets.

He was still wearing his wristwatch. I was struck by this fact. Most people put their watches aside long before entering this stage. I'm still wearing Ken's from the time he took his off, a full two days before the end.

A minute or so passed. He grew still. The wife and daughter hovered over the bed, one to a side, each holding one of his hands. There was a tape recorder propped on the pillow, and the daughter held the small recorder in her free hand. I stood at the foot of the bed, empty-handed.

Oh, the buildup! And then the letdown. Part of the problem was the way that breathing stops, stutters, starts up again, and how often it's impossible to tell — we seemed to have temporarily forgotten this — which moment is the last until it's over.

That's what Mr. Straughn was doing: stopping, starting. Maybe he was summoning himself back by main force to speak that final word. If so, he needn't have bothered. The word was never heard. Because he grimaced with effort — the labor of merely breathing, let alone trying to speak — his wife leaned in close and spoke in his stead. Drowned him out with "I love yous" and "Honey, we're here, right beside you. We won't leave you alone." She couldn't help herself, I'm not blaming anyone, but she might as well have stuffed his mouth with wads of cotton wool — cotton wool dipped in honey to seal it in tight. His mouth opened silently one last time. Stopped. So much effort, so little sound.

"Gone?" Vinnie asked, as I made my way back to the nurses' station. I nodded yes, since I couldn't get a word out. Then my eyes brimmed. It wasn't fair. Not Mr. Straughn's passing, which was expected, and as natural as could be under the circumstances, but the death of his project, when he'd planned so hard and come within an inch of carrying it out. And I, too, felt the poorer for that.

By now, the signs of approaching death are familiar to me. They vary so little. The legs are lost first, then the arms and the neck. Everything sags near the end: the earlobes flatten, lie close along the skull, the jaw goes slack, the head lolls, too heavy to lift; secretions pool and thicken in the throat; the fingers, before this so restlessly seeking, fold in, and are still. It's a relentless letting-go; and, finally, with bladder and bowels a surrender of any surviving shred of the illusion of control.

I know the outward signs as well as anyone. The mask. I see — I see whatever there is to see: blackout, suffocation, a great yawn — I see nothing, the blandest of nothings. I'm left in the kindergarten of understanding, piping my single question, over and over — is this *all?*

Mr. Straughn tried to remedy this, dying with his will clenched like a fist around the last fading ember of consciousness, not loosening his grip until his hand was forced.

And now he's gone, taking his secret with him. "Gone before," as they used to say, leaving not a chink, not the faintest seam of light, to show us where. Did he find out what he wanted to know? Or forget entirely what he set out to find?

For my part, I still can't help thinking of our lives as stories, journeys, handings-on. "Gone before" says it as well as anything. Maybe the dying person knows but cannot say, receives but cannot send. Mr. Straughn wanted to send, wanted desperately to say — if not whole words, then at least crumbs flung backwards as he went on ahead, so we wouldn't be so lost when the time comes for us to follow, as it surely must.

Sightings

"Cut the lace," Sue Manning would say. "I don't want any more valentines." Or once when, in Sue's opinion, Mary had really indulged herself: "Please! You're giving me diabetes." Sue would remind all her students for the umpteenth time that true art is tough-minded — "like tempered steel," and she'd quote the great story writer Isaac Babel: "No steel can pierce the human heart as chillingly as a period placed at the right moment." But all to no avail.

Mary Owen had been one of Sue's most hopeless students, and surely the most persistent she'd ever encountered. Year after year, she'd sign up for Sue's course, Creative Writing — Manning — 1, attending faithfully, absorbing nothing. She wrote of porch swings and summer romance, of secrets she'd never told anyone before but not worth hiding, ever, of courtship kisses so innocent they made you blush, of golden fields unspotted by aphid or wireworm. In the world as Mary found it, love was lovely, good prevailed, and death was perfect peace. She had a fondness, too, for certain antique words: "beholds," "pines for," "yearns." *Yearns!*—who on earth, Sue wondered, ever says that word anymore?

The course was something Sue gave as part of the continuing education program at the local junior college. She didn't *have* to do it — she had a full teaching load at a four-year college during the day. The extra pay was ridiculously small, but Sue figured it was a way of doing her bit for the community. And, often enough, it was a welcome change from sullen undergraduates suffering through the obligatory English Comp. It was a night course open to all; those who attended wanted to be there. They were adults, mostly in the twenty- to thirty-year-old range. Mary must have been in her late sixties, early seventies, old enough to be the mother of everyone in the class, including the instructor. It might have been simple loneliness that drew her to the class, but Sue guessed it was something more: that, despite all the evidence to the contrary, Mary felt she actually had something in her to say.

This semester, Mary signed up again but only attended three classes. It wasn't like her at all. Sue asked around and learned through the grapevine that Mary was in hospice, gravely ill. "Heart," they said, and Sue remembered thinking, Of course, it would be her heart . . .

Mary wasn't expected to last into summer, so Sue made a point of dropping in on her when she could. The first time Sue visited, she asked, none too imaginatively, whether Mary was still writing. Why not write about *this* — whatever she was going through? Mary shook her head, no, and gave a rather slanting smile. "Too much pain?" Sue asked. No, it wasn't that. "They're good about pain here," she said, "I'm too busy." Busy with *what*? Sue wanted to ask, but held herself back and bided her time. She waited in vain, though. Mary wasn't about to elaborate — at least not during that visit.

How could you be busy *in hospice*? It didn't make a scrap of sense to Sue Manning. Sue had never liked hospitals, but at least she knew what business they were in. What puzzled her about hospice was this: when the doctors say nothing more can be done, what substitutes for the doing? It was clear to Sue that the question revealed something about herself — she tended to be aggressively active and interfering, and would undoubtedly make a terrible patient when the time came.

She taught on Tuesday evenings, and tried to visit Mary on Wednesdays so that they could talk about the class if Mary felt like it. Why am I doing this? Sue often asked herself. They had nothing in common besides the class, yet it wasn't merely a duty call on Sue's part. She couldn't help liking Mary. And, too, something had gone from the class with Mary's departure, some resistance Sue had counted on being there, if only to push against. From time to time, when Sue would come out with something perfectly clear and reasonable to everyone else in the room, Mary would turn on Sue this look of wide-eyed astonishment. No question asked, no objection raised, not a word emitted, but a perfectly *speaking* gaze. Lately, Sue had begun to suspect that her class might be running along too smoothly; she feared that consensus might be making her soft.

The visit Sue would remember longest was on an evening of wild weather, everything bending or blowing, then ominously still. She was watching the news on television beforehand, not so much the news itself as the orange band at the bottom of the screen, a continuous ribbon of words gliding past: reports of funnel cloud sightings in Deaf Smith County, followed by TORNADO ALERT and the names of the affected counties, SWISHER, RANDALL, POTTER. Then: STAY TUNED. WE ARE CURRENTLY EXPERIENCING TRANSMISSION DIF-FICULTIES. Sue briefly considered staying home. Not that her house was so safe — she didn't have a basement — but, if a fun-nel cloud ever touched down, being out in an automobile was asking for it. She felt somehow that Mary was counting on the visit, though, and decided to risk it.

On the drive over, she tried to pick up some music on the radio, but it was the same thing there — *stay tuned, stay tuned* — warning beeps every other minute. Tips on hiding places: basements and closets were best. The sky was murky green — filthy, really — as though she were moving under the skin of a pond.

Everything looked slightly peculiar then. Like this kid floating a wire hanger in a paper sleeve out the window of a passing car, canting it like the wing of a plane. Then at one point, she remembered, the road emptied. The only other car in sight was the pickup in front of her. The driver was wearing a Stetson with an upturned brim — nothing unusual in that. But, that evening, the back of his head had become a startling sight: the brim in silhouette giving him horns, one curving up over each ear. Sue figured it was the eerie light that made everything strange, and her being tired on top of everything else. If the wind had been the least bit stronger, she probably would have turned back.

As she entered the hospice building, what struck her first was the quiet, the enveloping hush. It hadn't seemed noisy outside, but now she could tell it must have been. The entrance vestibule had no windows, so she felt she was safely out of the weather. Out of the world, really; the feeling of enclosure was very welcome to her at that moment. Then she spotted some Xeroxed signs taped to the walls — each with a big clumsily lettered *A*, unexplained. In the top inner triangle of the *A* was a squiggle made with a Magic Marker, a leaning corkscrew shape, meant to look like a twister, although if you hadn't known what was going on outside, it would have been anyone's guess what the shape signified. *A* stood for "Alert" — that had to be it — the tornado alert. Even here in hospice she wasn't going to be allowed to forget it.

One of the nurses stopped her at the desk, pushing forward a clipboard and pen. Being asked to sign in was something new. And it wasn't enough to sign her own name, Sue also had to spell out the name and room number of the person she'd come to visit. She couldn't refrain from making a comment on how rules and regulations seemed to be sprouting up all over the place recently.

"Oh, it's only for tonight," the nurse apologized.

"Why tonight?" Sue persisted.

"Well, you know," said the nurse.

And then Sue caught on: "You're taking a census, in case we blow away and you have to find us."

The nurse nodded. "Exactly right."

Mary was perched on top of the sheets when Sue entered. She was wearing a housecoat and slippers, both in cheerful shades of pink, and it seemed clear that she had no intention of staying in bed.

She greeted Sue warmly, as she always did, and confided that her visit came at the right time, she'd been feeling "itsy" all day.

"I think you mean 'antsy,'" Sue corrected her gently.

"*That's* the word I was looking for — yes." Mary smiled.

After that, Mary inquired, as she always did, how the class was coming along, what the students were writing about, who was doing the best work and what made it best. Then she wanted to show Sue some writing — not hers, no, her grandson's. He was seven. The document, a much-folded sheet of construction paper, was ready and waiting on the bed table. There were small, green flower faces around the borders.

"Dear Nana —" Sue read aloud. The letters were crayoned

red and green, all caps, with *R*'s reversed. The lines sloped upwards. "Come home please come. I hope you fill better soon. I
am sorry for this happen. I love you. to — Nana from — Clint"

"Only seven years old," Sue said admiringly. "He's very ad-
vanced for his age."

"Isn't he a wonder?" Mary agreed. "The precious!"

Sure enough, Mary gave no sign of being aware of the
weather situation. No reason she should have: the curtain was
closed, the television silent. You couldn't *feel* the wind in her
room. Still, Sue thought she could hear it, though muffled now,
the sound of water moving sluggishly, or of a giant bird circling
overhead, wings flailing.

Mary looked rather pale and peaked, more tired, though not
dramatically worsened from the last visit. Sue wanted to know
whether she felt up to taking a walk. Mary wasn't sure, but she
thought she'd like to give it a try. She'd had some bad moments
yesterday. Still — her doctor had urged her to keep on doing as
much as she could for as long as she could. So Sue fetched
Mary's three-pronged cane, helped her onto her feet, and together they set out.

Sue had resolved not to draw Mary's attention to the signs
on the walls, not to mention them unless she did. And Mary
did seem oblivious to them. The walk went very slowly, the
placing of one foot after the other, securing one, loosing the
other, seemed to require all her concentration. She'd made it
clear that she could manage without a helping arm, but Sue
walked close alongside. It struck Sue that Mary was scuffing
her feet along, not much lift to them. She'd done better last
visit.

They'd passed the nurses' station and made it halfway to the
end of the west corridor when Mary made a sudden lurch for
Sue's arm. It was plain she'd had enough. Back in her room,

Mary resisted returning to bed, though. She thought she still had enough energy to sit up for a while, and chose one of the visitors' armchairs. "It kinda hurts my feelings, not being able to take a real walk," she said.

Sue chose the sofa; Mary's empty bed stood between them, as if they were both visiting a third person. They sat on without speaking. Sue didn't know about Mary, but, for herself, she certainly didn't feel the need to be saying something every minute, to cram the spaces with small talk, as strangers would. They'd known each other for years, after all.

When the door to the hallway suddenly clapped shut, Mary smiled — why, Sue couldn't imagine right then. She sprang up and opened it, giving the doorstop a firm shove with her heel and an extra kick to test that it held. It did. While she was at it, Sue walked over to check whether the door to the courtyard was locked. Fine: everything tight.

There'd been no sound of wind in the hallway, but, back in the room, Sue could hear it again: this big rushing sound overhead, same as before. And something else this time, brushing against the outside of the window, stroking the glass. The window was shut tight, though, the heavy curtain did not stir. She wondered what the latest weather update might be but counted on the nurses coming and collecting them if conditions worsened. The corridors should be relatively safe, shielded as they were from windows.

"It's too exhausting." Mary sighed. "I've enjoyed about all I can tolerate."

Sue waited in silence for Mary to explain herself.

"You noticed the signs in the hallway?" Mary asked. She gave Sue one of her musing looks.

"As a matter of fact —"

"What do you think?"

"What do *you* think?" Sue asked.

"Well, *it's obvious,*" she said, "they're telling us the angels are here."

Sue's face must have spoken for her.

"I see you don't believe me."

Sue couldn't deny it: she didn't believe in angels. They made her a little angry in fact. Granted, she read and admired Rilke and Blake, and they were full of angels, but their angels were pure art. The assertion of belief, whether in dragons, devils, griffins, angels, or creatures of that ilk, was really irrelevant in a literary sense. The important thing was not whether Blake actually *saw* angels but what sort of poetry he made of the experience, whatever it was. In his case, first-rate poetry — all that mattered.

"Art, being bartender, is never drunk," a line of Peter Viereck's from — she forgot which poem — was a part of her teaching creed, along with Isaac Babel's bit about placing a period at the right moment. Add to that her unending battle against cliché — and angels, as Sue saw it, were fast becoming clichés. Indeed, they were becoming a lucrative business — think of all those Hallmark cards! Even the New Agers were cashing in. *Slews* of books — find your inner angel, ask your angel, answers from angels. . . . And where was it she'd seen on television . . . ? On some talk show or other this woman testifying that when her husband lost his job and they were forced to sell their house and move, what do you know, an angel appeared to her. She was watering her African violets — the angel flew out of the spout of her watering can. Genie-in-the-bottle sort of thing. And the angel told her where to relocate. And when they did relocate, the job was close by, waiting. Sue was very happy for the woman, but *please,* she thought, spare me! Tell it to the psychiatrist.

Then Sue realized that Mary was still staring at her.

"Penny for your thoughts," Mary said.

"About angels. I think they're the materialization of a wish, a desire —"

"I'm with you there." Mary nodded.

"But the materialization is self-induced."

"There," Mary said, "is where we differ. I never asked them to come to me. *They* desired — they invited themselves. And now that they've come, I wish they'd go away. Once was enough. It's too exhausting. They've made their point." She turned to Sue then, and asked so gently it didn't sound like a question: "You've never been visited, have you?"

"Never!" Sue sounded shocked.

Right then, as chance would have it, Sue heard a loud sigh coming from the open door, and she knew at once — but never how she knew — that it was the doorstop starting to slide. Too much! She lurched to her feet and threw herself against the door before it swung free. As Sue stood there, facing down the door (surely a ridiculous sight!), she had the distinct impression that Mary was waving behind her back — to someone sitting on the bed. She turned, her knuckles white on the knob. "Want this open or closed?"

"Guess it'd be easier if we kept it —" Mary clucked, trying to stifle a laugh. "Closed," she said. "Yes, better shut. You see how mischievous they are!"

This time she'd gone too far. Sue really felt provoked, and did what she'd resolved not to do — she started to blurt out the tornado news. "It's the wind," she began. "If you'd turn on your TV right this very minute, you'd see —"

"No need for television," Mary cut her short.

Startled by Mary's sudden self-assurance and having no heart to fight her, Sue never actually arrived at the word *tor-*

nado. Instead, she did something very hard for her: she resigned herself to listening. "Tell me what you've been seeing," she said.

"You won't laugh?"

Sue promised. It never had been a laughing matter, as far as she was concerned; on the contrary, the subject made her irritated.

"Well," Mary began. "They're different ones, you know, at different times. I've seen some pretty unfriendly. I think the first ones were best. I wanted to laugh — *with* them, not *at* them. And then I felt — I want to say 'peaceful,' but that isn't really the right word. A sense of abundance, I guess. The fullness of things seen and unseen . . . Scripture, you know. Am I making any sense to you?"

"Not a whole lot," said Sue. "There's something I've never been able to fathom: why would angels want to have anything to do with *us*? They're supposed to be perfect, and we're so obviously not. Anyway — it's too vague, what you're telling me. Remember what I kept harping on in class? Sights, sounds, tastes, textures, smells. Give it to me in those terms."

"Like I said, they were all different. . . ." Mary lifted her gaze, and her eyes tracked the ceiling for a moment, as if searching for traces she could point to. "So . . . all right. It's hard, but — you're probably stuck on an image you have of the wings. Or the gowns — or the harps — something like that. They're not important. So, first of all, I can't say anything about gowns or wings. Or even faces. No faces. Either I don't remember, or I never saw them. Sometimes all I can make out are shimmers of wavy air, like you see around a jet plane, you've seen those."

"That's due to heat, of course," Sue put in.

"Yes, of course. With the jet, it's heat. Only a simile. You draw the edges around things too tight, you know. Anyway . . . what was I saying? Oh yes, you wanted to know what they're like. It's never the same twice. They might look like flashes of light one time, quick and changing. One time they'll be perfectly quiet, the next, noisy as a swarm of bees. Hear *that*?"

Sue wondered then: had Mary been hearing the wind all along? At the time she first chose to make mention of it, the wind sounded to Sue's ears even softer than before.

"I know what you're thinking. . . . You think I've gone clear out of my head. But since you said you wanted to know what I saw, I'm trying, best I can, to tell you. How can I describe it?" She paused; Sue nodded encouragingly without speaking. Then Mary resumed.

"What I see mostly is feet, flashes of feet. I can't say whether they're men or women, it doesn't seem to matter in the least. Last night, I felt this tremendous *push* — pure mischief — and, it's true, I did fall, but I was pushed. Saw one swooping down, from that very corner" — she pointed to a patch of ceiling directly over Sue's head. "That very same corner you're looking at now, swooping down on me like he was swimming the breaststroke. And, once, but only that once, I saw one about as big as you are, which isn't very big, you know, with *huge* wings, spread from this wall to that" — she stretched out her arms, indicating the full breadth of the room — "wasn't doing anything but hovering there, wings beating. But that was the only time I saw wings. Mostly, like I told you, all I can see are the soles of their feet flashing by.

"You're going to think I've really lost my mind," she concluded.

She was right about that. Sue thought Mary had finally plunged off the deep end, yet the experience, whatever it was, seemed to have been good for her. Sue could see the tiredness,

the eye hollows deepened with pain, but also something else —
not a brightness, quite, but a clarity — something unclouded in
her expression. Sue knew she was waiting for her to speak.

"Well" — Sue struggled — "that's really interesting . . . I
only wish you'd written with the same kind of imagination
when you handed in your class assignments. But what I still
can't grasp is: what does all this say to you?"

"You're asking what the meaning is — what angels *mean?*"
Sue nodded.

Mary answered quickly, as though the meaning were obvious. "Why, that we're not alone, see? That I won't be left in
darkness. Look — I know you don't believe me, but promise
again that you won't laugh —"

Sue reminded her that she hadn't laughed before.

"Try to think of it this way." Mary studied her lap, avoiding
Sue's eyes. Sue was trying her best to keep her expression neu-
tral, receptive. "Angels mean . . . how can I put it? Well . . .
pathways." She dragged to a halt. Then she started up again.

It made, as Sue found herself saying whenever she told the
story afterwards, "almost no sense," and that equivocating
"almost" breathed itself out with a little crash of surprise,
every time. To be exact: it made no sense to Sue then, and
makes almost no sense to her now, but it never occurred to
her to laugh at what Mary said next, then or now. "Pathways . . ." — she turned her full gaze upon Sue — "coming
and going. I dream of wings to fly away from my bed—they
dream of walking on feet. Not a word is said — they just go
on by, flashing the soles of their feet. And so I know . . . the
spirit yearns to put down feet."

Isolation

I F you pray," Father Martin strikes up his theme for the visit, "something will come." His words, consonants blunted, blister obscurely within his domed mask. "Pray" might be "play" or "fray," though probably not.

"There's an old saying, and it's true," he continues to harp, "you can't get an answer to a question you haven't asked."

There's a maddening symmetry to everything the priest says. Michael stares blankly at the voice-emitting mask; it's flesh colored, smooth, a mouth sewn up and healed over. Michael's tiring, his mind wanders, even a very short visit tires him out.

Father Martin urges Michael to think of this time in his life as a "teething of the spirit." Is that "teething"? Or "seething"? Michael doesn't ask him to repeat the word; either way, it's way off the mark. This kind of dying does not spiritualize — has nothing to do with spirit. Far from it: Michael feels he is being sucked into a deep, lightless swamp, a realm of filth and defilement. He's been incontinent for most of the week, diapered in paper, shit-soaked. Already mired in mud.

"I'm going to leave you with this." Father Martin places a small book bound in red on the blanket that covers Michael's diminished lap. It's a book of psalms, titled in gold. Michael receives it, murmurs his thanks. "Start anywhere," Father Martin proposes, yet his hand can't resist riffling the pages to where a marker already happens to rest.

Michael turns his head to stare out the window as the priest leaves. The curtains are partway open onto a sky of brass.

Father Martin closes the door carefully behind him. He jiggles the knob to make sure it is solidly shut.

Michael fingers the psalter, weighs the thing in one outstretched palm, but does not trouble to open it yet.

He lies alone in his slot of a bed, the bed in a slot of a room. It's April, past the middle of the month, moving along. He doesn't know the number attached to the day, this particular day, but he's not out of his mind yet, he can still tell time by the hour: five after three.

Alone. There's an isolation sign on the door — two signs, actually — Michael noticed when he was first wheeled in. He's in double isolation: Contact and Respiratory, that's how the warnings read. There's a small table beside the door to his room, holding protective gear: masks, gloves, gowns, towels, special red plastic disposable bags, and ties. Back in one of his earlier hospitalizations, a nurse tried to smooth things over by explaining to Michael that all these precautions were by way of "reverse isolation — protecting *you* from contamination by *us*." She thought the "reverse" part would soften matters, but it hardly made a difference. Call it what you like: it comes to the same thing. Gloved and masked, the nurses come and go. A doctor. A priest. The nights are long, phrases haunt him. *Gone to his rest. Eternal rest.* He's afraid of sleep, of being stuffed into that sack, of his mind struggling in darkness.

For two nights running, the same dream, its meaning so obvious that Michael suspects it isn't a dream at all but one of those mind movies that reels on incessantly, day and night, and tends to be unnoticed in the light. In this dream, or whatever, he's been thrown overboard. There's dancing on deck, orange lanterns strung to the rails like fruit on a vine. The water is inky and cold. The boat churns onward, cutting a white wake, carrying away its music and lights. Michael spurts forward, fast as he can, hollering after it. It's no use — hard as he pumps, the boat always slips out of reach, gliding ahead, serenely on course. He's eating water, knows he can't last. Hears the priest whisper, "Bite down on this," bites, he's biting — gulps of water — He's going down —

Michael has wakened each time, fingers harrowing the sheets as though he's been swimming in fact. He's desolate, inconsolable. Thrown overboard — that's exactly how it feels, but the part about dancing is strange, his yearning to join them. He doesn't dance. Has never wanted to dance.

And endured his first, and only, high school dance from the sidelines, splayed against the wall in an exaggerated at-ease, trembling hands clenched behind his back, his bowels churning. Even now, more than a decade later, he can still feel the fear. Battle fear, animal fear — but why? As if he were being hunted down. The dancing couples, gliding, leaning into each other, blurred before his eyes. He had no desire to join them, only to cut and run. Something — the tense, fake smile he'd pasted to his face, the bloated music, amplified to sweep them away, drowning out every other sound, the perfumes, the fumes of the flowers, all those corsages — choked him. So he'd fled — rejoicing — first to the lavatory, then to the parking lot, preferring, it seemed, exhaust-fouled air.

He always recalled feeling "different." Being studious, for one thing. His way of gazing off into the middle distance when people came too close. Growing up in West Texas with no interest in athletics, hot rods, girls, or guns, he'd been out of the swing of things for a long time. Then there'd been that final, isolating difference, and a secret, violent crush on his high school drama teacher — a married man.

His parish priest, Father Dennehy, told his parents that perhaps what they had was a young man with a religious calling, and his parents had been willing to consider the possibility; maybe this was the name of the difference everybody seemed to sense. Michael knew better, though, and as soon as he graduated, shook off the dust of West Texas and headed for the coast. He'd never had any problems about taking whatever job came up. In his spare time, he started acting in a community theater in Sacramento; there, he met Thomas, fell in love, came to feel, for the first time ever, not different, not alone.

After Thomas went home to Boston to die, Michael hadn't the heart to start over. Thomas belonged to one of the "good, old families," that's how Michael's only letter (from the sister) put it. The letter forbade Michael to communicate with Thomas in any way. How was it said? Thomas would "not be heard back from. . . ." Something like that. Michael only read the letter once, then tore it to shreds. Thomas's sister had been as good as her word the one time Michael had tested her by phoning. Consistent to the end: even the obituary notice, clipped from a parish newsletter, was sent to him weeks after the funeral —

When his own disease had progressed from "indolent" to "fulminant," as the doctor so memorably put it, he'd taken his mother up on her invitation to "come back home." And so he had come — back to the place he'd fled, the home he'd never thought of as home. To his friends in California, he'd "checked out," "dropped off the edge of the earth." Houston, Dallas,

even Austin, were charted, on the map of the land of the living — but Amarillo? The letters and postcards which followed
at first gradually dried up. Michael had expected this, wasn't
really surprised. And, anyway, there was no more fight in him.
Then came his mother's stroke, and Michael, no longer ambu-
latory himself, needed to be cared for professionally, and finally, taken in.

> *Let them vanish like water that runs away*
> *Like grass let them be trodden down and wither.*

The psalter isn't helping.

The mind movies and dreams keep on coming. Some tease,
some frighten. Some have narratives; some don't — are mere
eyefuls, or earfuls. The latest, an urgent one, is only a voice.
Whose? It seems pretty strange to Michael that he can't recognize whose voice it is. Maybe the radio announcer on the early
morning news, he thinks, that's one possibility. He has no radio
now to check on this. Still — identifying the voice isn't the
point, he's evading the point. The words are what count; they
are clear and distinct: ". . . or we can just plant you, if you prefer."

Michael does not prefer. No time to waste now; he's mucked
around long enough. Confess. Receive the sacraments. Plan the
funeral. Make whatever peace.

Michael has confessed and received absolution according to
the rite. He can now receive Communion, but he doesn't feel
up to it right yet. Nor is he ready to be anointed. Not yet.

Absolved, Michael feels nothing but emptiness, as if his sin
had been his last connection to the world.

"How do you feel?" Father Martin wants to know. He talks

too much, asks too many questions. It's as if the mask, by canceling his mouth, compels him to speak.

Feel? In a word? There is no word. Michael turns his head away and stares out the window, surprised by the sudden ooze of tears. He's been on drops for days, artificial tears, his eyes so dry, so wept out.

There's weather out there, other side of the glass. Branches wrung by the wind. A wind that is soundless. Father Martin, shattering the silence, starts to say, "I think I know how you feel —"

"You don't and you *can't* —" Michael lashes back. "Don't hand me that!"

Father Martin answers softly, "I can understand why you're angry." He is not to be put off, though, and after a short pause, offers another of his texts. "The time of deepest despair is when hope enters us," he says, "only then are we empty enough." And then he points to the figure on the wall. Without commentary this time, he simply points.

Alone again, Michael eyes the figure on the cross warily; the little metal Christ suspended there is way too calm. Only the eyeholes in his hands weep. Mostly it's the prettiness that puts Michael off. The polite drapery, the fig leaf for modesty's sake — it's a lie. The nakedness is important; for this particular shame, Michael feels sure of it, was also a wound, not the least of his wounds.

Michael turns his face to the door as it opens and shuts. It's Father Martin, wearing his muzzle.

No, he isn't up to being anointed today. Michael feels the priest's sharp disappointment. That's why Father Martin is going on and on about how the rite has changed its name from "Extreme Unction" to "Anointing of the Sick." Michael can see that the new name sounds less scary and less final. But, call it what you wish, he isn't ready. "Tomorrow," he promises. And the funeral — while they're at it, they'd better talk about the funeral, tomorrow.

Father Martin asks about Michael's prayer life. "Anything happening?" he probes very gently. Michael shakes his head. He's reading the psalms, Michael tells him, scanning, tuning in and out. Wherever a phrase or a line seems to come to life for him. Any other way, he can't concentrate at all. "And when it comes to life?" Father Martin's voice lifts hopefully. Michael shrugs. He feels like he's hobbling on his knees towards something, but has no idea what.

Then the priest says something that sounds preposterous to Michael: "In your isolation, in your suffering, there's a gift for you. Only you can unwrap it."

Raving!

> *You have noted my lamentation*
> *Put my tears into your bottle*
> *Are they not recorded in your book?*

Michael tries to pray by moving his lips while reading the psalms. He tries waiting, listening, in silence. Nothing comes. Nothing but the usual: the night nurse, the day nurses, the doctor, mind movies, dreams. And the priest again.

Today, Father Martin has brought along a Bible, hymnal, and a book of rites. He opens the book of rites to the rubric Mass of Resurrection. Then he opens the hymnal to the index section. What to sing, what to say are the questions before them. Occasionally, in the past, Michael has thought about such things, but now they are matters of indifference to him. He won't be there for it to matter to him. It's also true that he doesn't want to be "just planted" — but if he's not going to be there, what's the difference?

Somehow, it does make a difference.

They settle on one of the standard texts, a passage concerning baptism and resurrection in Romans. Michael dwells on the line "Death has no more power over him." Let it be so.

And they pore over the approved list of choices for songs: "O God, Our Help in Ages Past," "The Strife is O'er, the Battle Done," "Saints of God, Come to His Aid". . . . What Michael really wants is "Ubi Caritas," a song he once loved and hasn't heard in ages. But there's bound to be someone (if anyone comes) who'd question the appropriateness of *caritas* in this case. Michael decides not to bring it up. "I leave it to you," he says, turning the choice over to Father Martin. He simply hasn't the energy.

They've actually made progress this session. Michael can see that Father Martin is pleased, even though he's still not ready to be anointed. Tomorrow, maybe. Father Martin has brought Holy Communion if Michael wishes to receive today. Michael does, but asks for only a piece of the Host. "Very small," he says. Father Martin promises. Removing his right-hand glove, he breaks off a morsel of consecrated bread for Michael. But the fragment of Host lies heavily on Michael's tongue while he tries to reconstruct how the act of swallowing is accomplished. Michael blinks and blinks until the ability is restored to him. He hadn't realized before now that swallowing was a sacrament as well.

Nor how famished he was.

Michael's losing count. His days, as well as his nights, continue ever more shapelessly, unpunctuated by meals, or neat alternations of sleeping and waking. There are some regularities:

the repeated humiliation of being wiped and washed, diapered and turned, the continuous burbling and swishing of humidifier and fan, the eyedroppered morphine, like clockwork, every four hours. Against this background, the slightest departure from routine, an almost-nothing, becomes something: an event.

It comes in the small hours of the morning. Long after midnight, anyway — Michael doesn't check the clock, he's too disconcerted, surprised. The phone rings, and Michael, sound asleep for once, shudders into wakefulness. He's shocked. He gropes for the receiver but, by the time he connects with it, the ringing stops.

Minutes later, Michael isn't at all sure of what it was that woke him. Don't they screen calls here? They must. He's not about to ask or complain, though. Surely, it's a mistake; he doesn't think he's dreamed it. He places the phone within reach before he allows himself to fall back to sleep.

They must have upped the morphine; Michael drifts off easily and sleeps heavily, sleeps and dreams. No frantic swimming for rescue this time; if anything, the pace is sluggish. What's really strange is that his dream is announced beforehand, like a formal visitor. His night nurse, Nan, opens the door, stands on the threshold, and says: "It's ———," a name he doesn't catch.

Another thing about this dream: it almost allows him to dance. In the dream, Michael is watching the backs of the ushers at church, those backs that had always struck him as so righteously, self-consciously, rigid. They are bending and straightening now, taking up the collection, guiding the long-poled tithing baskets down the length of the pews. Plowing the furrows. Reaching, stretching, contracting, returning. . . . Michael is following one of the backs down the street. Buttocks and back — the man is tall. Cut into the leather of his belt is the name RULF. Now they are in an embrace, Michael and Rulf, rubbing against each other, scraping, abrading. "Should we?" Rulf whispers. There's sand in the cracks of his teeth, in the corners of his lips, in the hairs of his mustache. When Rulf bends for a kiss, Michael notices, for the first time, that the leaf of his ear is torn —

Michael knows no one, has never known anyone, who goes by the name of Rulf, nothing even close. Not even a Ralph. The sandy mustache could only be Thomas, though. He doesn't have time to ponder this because the phone is ringing again — it's what awakened him. This time, Michael manages to snatch the receiver to his ear before the cutoff. He presses the speaking end to his mouth but says nothing. From the other end: an answering nothing, a pause of maybe a minute. Then the sound of breathing. The click of disconnection. The dial tone.

All too quiet after this.

Although there are no further interruptions, Michael has trouble falling back to sleep. He has almost no bodily cushioning now; lying on his back, even while shifting his weight from buttock to buttock, is becoming actually painful. When he was back at his mother's house and couldn't sleep, he'd ease the tension by touching the wall, walking his fingers up and down the smooth surface, but here at hospice, however far he stretches his arm, he can't reach any of the walls. No wonder he feels adrift. Unable to fall back to sleep on his own, Michael presses the call button and asks to be turned. After being turned, he asks for more pain medication. His heart labors, he can hear it. In the silence that surrounds him now, it sounds unnaturally loud.

Open your mouth and I will fill it

Tuesday. Michael is now making a point of repeating the name and number of the day. *April 24.* Sometimes he asks the nurse to write it out for him so he won't forget. Today is Tuesday, April twenty-fourth, a day without event. Except for when a bird crashes against the window glass and drops. The bird falls silently, not a cheep is heard. Michael can't raise himself by himself to see what's happened to the creature. By the time he gets a nurse to check, she tells him nothing's fallen, there's nothing on the ground.

Late in the afternoon, Father Martin visits. "And how's the prayer life?" he asks first thing. "Still trying," Michael answers. "Maybe you're trying too hard," Father Martin says. And, once again, he reflects: "Waiting and listening are also ways . . ."

"Oh, I'm listening," Michael puts in. "That's good," Father Martin says. He speaks to Michael about God coming in ways you never expect. Michael nods and holds his peace.

Except for the nurses, Father Martin is the only person to enter Michael's room today. Today, Tuesday, April twenty-fourth. Michael's shaky as water, knows he's weaker. And that's all his news for the day, should anyone ask.

Before settling for the night, Michael places the phone on his bed, within easy reach. There are no calls. He sleeps more soundly than the night before but wakes in a darker mood. Clearly, the calls last night must have been for the wrong number, a mistake that's now been corrected.

Wednesday. April 25. The lady in the red shoes visits. Joann, is it? He keeps misplacing her name. Sharon and Terry, the day nurses, come and go. Dr. Danner. Father Martin doesn't show, and there are no calls that night. Michael has placed the phone back on the bed table, but he keeps the bed table close, in case.

Nothing. Or, wait — something. Twice. This: the sound of tires being scrubbed on a too-tight curve, then a car horn. Somebody leaning on the horn. Or maybe it's stuck. Michael's never heard any noises filtering in from the street before this. No words from the outside until now. These aren't really words, though, he has to remind himself.

Michael pushes the call button for the night nurse; he needs a change of position. By grabbing a bed rail and, by leaning and pulling on it, he's pleased to be able to assist Nan in turning him without her having to call another nurse for assistance. Soon after Nan leaves, though, he feels like he's been parked and left on the side of a hill. He's so uncomfortable that he has to ring for her again. His pillow is drenched with sweat.

Thursday. April 26. Michael is anointed. Father Martin peels off his right glove to apply the consecrated oil. Michael stares out the window afterwards: the sky today like flint. A telephone cable stretches from the outer wall above his window to some point beyond the frame. Within the frame: A web of tree branches. Bench. Bird feeder. Gate.

Michael is suffering from severe air hunger today. He's conscious of each breath he draws — it's short of what he needs.

Night. He waits the darkness through. Saliva thickens, a sludge, in his throat. He swallows, coughs, swallows. . . . If he stops coughing, he's afraid he'll forget how to swallow. If he doesn't swallow, how will he breathe?

But Michael does breathe, and the phone catches him sleeping. He lifts the receiver on the third ring, before the caller has time to hang up. He's greeted by silence. Enough of this tease! He blurts out: "Hello. Hello? Who's there?"

Nothing answers at first. Then, something: a rustling of cloth, followed by the heavy suggestive breathing of an obscene caller. Michael repeats his question: "Who *are* you?" Is answered by the click of disconnection, the dial tone. He uses his remote to switch on the wall light and check the time. A few minutes after two.

Michael doesn't know what to make of the call — crossed wires, a number misdialed, a mischievous operator? A sick joke? Or part of a dream? Maybe the sound he was hearing was the sound of his own breathing amplified. Maybe the dream was a way of telling him that he was having trouble breathing and had better wake up and raise his head. Could be that he'd started to wake with his calling out: "Hello. Who's there?", that the dream scrambled the sequence, so that what he was doing was waking (in the dream), lifting the phantom receiver, and hearing phantom sounds (or his own breathing, distanced), and then waking for real. Whatever — the simple fact that he can analyze the possibilities reassures Michael that his mind is still clear.

But — two in the morning! He was sleeping before, and now he doesn't think he'll be able to drift off again. He lies on his back, making a tent of the sheet with his raised knees. The bony knobs of his knees. He runs a hand along his left shank: it's wasted, thigh and calf now seem to be nearly the same thickness. He is all bone.

Nothing to be done but stare up at the darkness. But even the darkness is unstable, drifting and flecked. Michael considers ringing for more Ativan to calm him but thinks, No, I've got to get a handle on this, on my own, the panic is in my mind. It's as if someone's turned up the amplification everywhere: he's acutely aware of the ticking of the clock, the burbling of the humidifier, the beating of his heart. He imagines he can actually hear the incessant small circlings of his mind, like a broom sweeping . . .

They've upped the morphine even more. Morning passes. Evening, another day. Saturday. Michael is restless, suffering from severe air hunger again. He's drowsing, though, when Father Martin stops by. Father Martin blesses him, tiptoes out. Michael wakes at the sound of the door closing.

The call comes shortly after midnight. It's the heavy breather, and already the joke is heavy, stale, it's been going on for too long. It sounds like the breather is practicing scales, scaling a ladder of breaths. The ladder is steep. Michael doesn't attempt to speak — wouldn't know what to reply, even if he did have breath enough to spare for it. It's a revelation to him how much breath the act of speaking requires. First, enough to form a bolus, from which the word is carved, then the favoring wind. Even if Michael were able to bring up the first breath shaping the word, he couldn't summon the added breath needed to launch it.

Another call comes after two. The same practical joker, Michael is sure of it, the same tired old joke — why bother to pick it up?

But he does pick it up, and it isn't the same.

What he hears is a pulse of compression and release, then the rush of many strong birds — what must be the surge of the telephone cable itself, the dense gabble of many voices interwoven in one. It's a sound he remembers from walking down country roads, the summer before he first left home. He was so restless, he couldn't wait to be gone from West Texas, he was ready to go. There were open fields on either side, a telephone cable stitching the air high overhead. The wire went on, humming with secrets it wasn't yet telling, bound for elsewhere, where he, too, was going —

When morning comes —

His head does not turn when the priest enters. Father Martin finds Michael lying on his back and leaning a little to one side. He bends over the bed, searching Michael's unshut eyes for

expression, for any sign of meeting, sorrow, protest, or surprise. Nothing — the shine is gone. Nothing but the usual, utterly mysterious face of the newly dead: the open mouth
stopped in full cry — shouting, singing, anybody's guess.

Father Martin prays his good-bye and Godspeed — "Lord,
remember him in your kingdom . . ." — then continues to
stand at the side of the bed, saying nothing at all. Touches his
hand to Michael's forearm and rests it there. Not yet cool:
through the thin film of rubber, he can still feel the fever.

Shutting the door carefully behind him on his way out, a line
from — where? Is it Scripture? — comes mockingly to mind:
"Remember to close the gates."

Father Martin pauses at the utility table. Absently, he pushes
the flesh-colored mask up over his nose and eyes, where it sits
on his brow like a tumor or an extra forehead. He opens one of
the folded disposal bags. Neatly peels off left glove, right glove.
Recollects the mask and plucks that off, roughing up his hair in
the process. Ties the disposal bag tight and drops it into the
lined container provided. Glances back once, questioningly,
over his shoulder, to the door with the double warning notice
on it, as he makes his way on down the hall to the nurses' station.

He finds Vinnie all by herself at the desk. She takes one
glance at his face before saying, "I think I know what you're
going to say, Father," before he's had time to get a word out.
"You have to understand what kind of night it's been. Two
new admissions late yesterday afternoon, a death right before
the early morning shift came on. And now, Michael . . ."

She pages Michael's nurse on the intercom. Words are
exchanged — blurted, really. Then she turns back to Father
Martin: "Sharon's on her way. She'll pronounce him. We're
short-staffed today on top of everything else. It's hard to be —

just a sec —" As if to prove her point, the phone and the inter-com start shrilling at the same minute. Father Martin stares blankly at the clergy sign-in book until Vinnie's free to turn back to him.

"Back to Michael," Vinnie resumes. "Yes, Michael," Father Martin says. "It's a mercy, really," Vinnie says. Father Martin doesn't dispute this.

"He had a restless night. More restless than usual, I should say; he's never been what you'd call peaceful. And," Vinnie adds, "we knew he was active, but we didn't know how long. . . . But the strange thing was — when Nan went in about three in the morning to check on him, she found him sound asleep and clutching the phone. I can't think who could have been calling — we've got a very short list of names for him, and none of them ever got in touch. I've seen a few dying alone — mostly old ones — never anybody so young. Nan said he was holding the receiver to his chest. 'Like a bouquet,' she said, 'like he was showing off something precious he'd been given,' and she had all she could do to pry it loose from his grasp."

Leaning

LOUELLEN HAD BEEN long enough on the job by then to have seen Evelyn Farley's case all the way from admission to — what she assumed was — the end. Talk about stress — forty-three days of all of them sitting around waiting!

Trouble with the Farley family surfaced right at the start. Abe Farley, the patient's husband, refused to sign any of the admission papers, although the doctors at the hospital had explained that there was nothing more they could do, and had turned the patient over to hospice. One of the hospital administrators had approved the transfer, and someone in the family must have agreed to it — enough to start the process, at least. But, here, it ground to a halt. Everything waited on the arrival of the daughter Nell, who was tied up right then. All the nurses could do was to cool their heels and hope that nothing drastic happened in the meantime. Nell did arrive, about an hour later, and only then did the admission go forward.

Louellen never did believe that Mr. Farley's balking was because he couldn't read — that was his son's story. She thought the old man well knew what those documents contained. It was the giving up he couldn't bear. He kept on asking what the "treatment plan" would be. That kind of language was a give-away, letting them know that Mr. Farley had been around hospitals for a long time.

To be fair, there'd been no time for the hospital to prepare them properly — the nurse had just gotten Mrs. Farley to bed, and taken some vital signs and a sample of blood, when they were told that everything was over. As far as the family was concerned, she'd been well enough to lay out the breakfast dishes the night before going into the hospital, so how sick could she be? She'd been in the hospital scarcely an hour before she got "traded" — Mr. Farley's word. He couldn't get over the fact that there wasn't going to be any more surgery, radiation, or chemo, only drugs for masking the pain. Sure, they'd been given a choice, hospital or hospice, but what could they do? All the doctors seemed to be in cahoots on this, making the same point about keeping her "comfortable," but no one in the family, least of all Mr. Farley, ever got used to the idea.

He was a picture, the Mister. Overalls and John Deere cap every day of the week. Could have been bald — Louellen never once saw him bareheaded. Yet, despite his getup, he had great dignity, a certain bearing. It had something to do with his posture, the way he squared his shoulders and the lift of his spine, his stiffness, and his silence. He'd sit for days on end at his wife's side, the family in circles around the old couple, the children in the first ring, with the grandkids tumbling and squabbling in the outer circle. One of the little tykes would break through the lines from time to time and toddle up to his grandmother. He'd stand beside her, tiny fingers working, trying to pry his grandmother's stiff fingers apart, certain she was hiding a candy for him. Nobody moved or said a word to stop him. Mr. Farley didn't even seem to notice; he'd sit there at his wife's side, the two of them at the center of it all. Both were motionless, wrapped in silence. Only once or twice did Mrs. Farley give any show of recognition to those around her. She was mainly comatose, in that limbo where you couldn't say she was dead, but it was hard to think of her as truly alive. She was in no pain, and already seemed far beyond caring.

At times, Louellen would wonder what the old man was thinking. Or what he saw when he stared out the window, for the curtains were often drawn back. Louellen thought that if she'd been staring for hours on end, day after day, at the same dreary patch of yard, the scene would begin to seem painted on the glass, less and less real as the vigil wore on. When, on a rare occasion, Mr. Farley unstuck himself from his chair, and started to walk down the hall, he seemed to be moving in a dream. And he'd usually manage to lose his way. He had his own health worries — respiratory problems, hearing loss, maybe a touch of Alzheimer's, too. Louellen wasn't sure how much Nell or any of his other children had known about his condition before this — his wife must have covered for him. Whenever Louellen asked him the name of a grandchild, he fumbled. Couldn't come up with a single one. "The wife knows," he said. "She could name ever' last one. I get 'em all mixed up." He knew the numbers, anyway: seventeen, with two more on the way.

Louellen found it best to reintroduce herself every time she had dealings with Mr. Farley, and he'd go through the introduction as if for the first time. She'd say "Louellen," and he'd ask her to repeat it, and she would, but he'd only catch the second half of the name, and that half must have blurred in his hearing. So she'd be "Ellie" to him for however little time he happened to remember. Wasn't ever long.

Nell was the only one you could connect with, the only one you could call the least bit talkative, and then, only in spurts —

when something really got next to her. Whatever Louellen learned came from her — the odd bits of family history, along with the family flavor.

Maybe *flavor* wasn't the word for it. What Louellen was trying to put a name to was their way of not quite facing you when they talked. Of not showing or saying what must have been on their minds. Even Nell had this faraway look whenever the talk got serious or close. She'd stare clear past Louellen to the end of the hall and beyond, like a driver with a destination in mind and a far stretch of road yet to go.

Mrs. Farley must have had that same look on her face when she first broke the news of her cancer. Nell was at the wheel, as she recalled it, her mother in the passenger seat beside her. They were at mile marker 62 on the Alton road, heading west. Louellen could see it all too clearly: the two of them staring at the road, facing *it,* not each other, the sun in their eyes. Nell might have reached over to tilt the visor down on her mother's side, but that would have been the extent of her reaching. Nell said she was too "embarrassed" to do anything but keep on driving. "It gives me kind of a headache sometimes," she admitted. "You know? All the things we never got around to saying? This humongous pressure — right *here,*" and she fingered the back of her neck.

Days passed, the wait wore on. Everybody on the staff would be asking: "How long can she keep on?" But, with the family, it was something else, like they were starting to think maybe she'd make it, after all. All of them were gazing down the same road, but what the staff and the family saw ahead of them was different entirely. The nurses tried not to discourage the family, but refused to give grounds for any false hopes. They did their best to keep Mrs. Farley dry and comfortable, and, mainly, they succeeded — she never got bedsores. They'd change her position every two hours or so, and stretch her limbs — all but her left leg, which was locked in a bent position. And they'd adjust her five pillows, one between the knees, one under each arm, two at the head. They kept her well covered up — there was more and more wasted flesh. Sometimes Louellen would offer ice cream to the little ones who showed up every day. One of the grandkids — her name escaped Louellen, Sally, she thought, or Cindy, anyway she was cute as a button — took her first steps and learned to walk in the hallway between rooms 118 and 112, with most of the staff cheering her on.

The end came on a Tuesday. It happened peacefully, as they'd expected: the woman simply stopped breathing. There'd been no unusual signs earlier that day, so Fern decided it was time to give Mrs. Farley a whirlpool bath — she'd been getting only bed baths for the past week. They lifted her onto the bath cart, heaped her up with blankets and towels, and wheeled the cart down the hall. Then peeled the coverings off, lowered the cart, and set the whirlpool whirling. And Mrs. Farley simply slipped away.

Fern thought what happened was that she couldn't let go with everybody sitting there and watching her like that, so the bath gave her the privacy she needed.

Cleaned and dried and into her hospital gown, they laid Mrs. Farley back on her bed again, straightened her, all but the knee. Fern pointedly left the side rails down. She alerted the desk on their way back, and Sharon soon joined them. It was Sharon who took blood pressure and pulse, listened for heart sounds, for breath sounds, examined her eyes, and then pronounced her. There was a terrible chill in the room right then. The family was very quiet — very upset. Hurt that she'd taken leave of them on her own. Nell finally let loose with what must have been on all their minds: here it had been touch-and-go for so long now, with the whole family waiting at her side "to make sure she wouldn't be alone . . ." And, here, Nell lost it. Couldn't say another word.

Sharon tried to tell them how often this happens, the patient holding on and holding on until the watchers step outside for a minute, and the patient, in that exact same minute, allows herself to let go. "That, too," she explained, "is one way of showing love."

They heard her out in such stony silence that Sharon hesitated before she moved to Nell and offered one of her well-practiced hospice hugs. Then the family once more drew its own circle around Mrs. Farley — drew in tight. Nell reached for the hand of her brother; the rest, staring at their feet or the bed, shyly linked hands. Nell started singing the hymn, and their voices joined together, swelled up. Fern and Sharon felt comfortable standing there singing along with the family, but Louellen didn't. It was too much — she felt so stretched today, why? This death was a mercy, long awaited. But she had to get away.

They were well into "Lean on Jesus" as Louellen passed through the door. Halfway down the hall, she still could hear them. It was that first refrain, that double "Lean — ing . . . Lean — ing . . ." One deep voice, breaking, stopping, starting up and breaking again, wasn't even trying to blend with the melody. Louellen knew whose voice it was.

Back at the nurses' station, Vinnie and Louellen waited for Nell to emerge. They were counting on her to handle things, as she'd done before. They weren't wrong in this. She did step out to ask "what next?" and Vinnie brought up the question of final arrangements. "The Simpsons do nice work," Vinnie suggested, "want me to call them?" Nell bit her lip, nodded. "Is that it?" she asked. "For now," Vinnie said, and Nell headed back to the room.

While Vinnie was occupied with talking to the funeral home, Louellen decided to set the tub room to rights. In all the confusion, they'd left the tub full of water, the whirlpool going. Even after Louellen reversed the lever, the water kept on churning. The plug was wedged in too tightly to come free by tugging on the cord, and Louellen had to dig for it, down into that warm, beating water. What had she gotten herself into? Hoping to forget her own hurt, she'd come to work at hospice, and here she was, plunged to her elbows, awash in sorrow.

It was so weird, the water went on rustling, rumbling. Circles — they looked like mouths — formed on its surface, amplified and faded. Voices came back to her. "He called me his honey . . . his honey," whispered the woman with the beautiful rings. "I'm dying, I don't care." It was the difficult patient in 115, nobody's favorite. Louellen bowed her head, tears springing. It had been so long, holding her breath, it felt, her first tears since — when was it? Weeks back — ages ago. Not since she made a spectacle standing out in the street, kicking and hollering, beating up on her car. Then, she'd wept for anger and shame — for herself. This was different, not for herself especially, though she, too, was included, this could swallow her, she might not come back . . . if she let it. But, no, she shook her head sharply. Straightened; grabbed for an unused towel, scrubbed face and hands with rough strokes until she was dry. Oh, more than dry. She kept her eyes on the open door. Somebody? No, nobody. Nobody saw. The water quieted, seeped away. It was over.

By the time Louellen had disinfected the tub and the bath cart, gathered up all the wet linen, and wheeled it down the hall, she could hear someone pulling up at the loading dock, which happened to be next door to the disposal room. The bell rang — she answered it. And there it was: the unmarked gray van from Simpson's. It was much too soon. Had it been a county burial, Louellen thought, they'd have taken their own sweet time about it. And they wouldn't have bothered with a fancy spread — any old blanket to hide what was under would do.

There was no way she could stop him, though, or slow him down. He'd already unfolded the long legs of what he liked to call his cot — a gurney dolled up with a maroon velvet cover. Vinnie tried to delay him when he checked in at the nurses' station, but even she couldn't do a thing. When Louellen glanced up next, he was standing outside the door to Mrs. Farley's room. Sharon wasn't far behind him. And Louellen decided to go back up there, give her a hand.

Mrs. Farley's children weren't ready yet, they wanted a few more minutes with the body — what could Sharon do but say "of course"? She suspected Mr. Farley wanted more time because he thought his wife might start up breathing again. Sharon figured the best thing was to leave him to see for himself.

So Sharon stepped out into the hall and tried to communicate all this to the man from Simpson's. Told him, too, that after the family was finished the staff still had some checking up to do. The man nodded agreeably — he was always agreeable. Louellen had found plenty of occasion to observe him before this. He was a specialist in not making a stir. But his manner irked Louellen right then.

Yet all he did was stand there, waiting on his moment, his gurney behind him, flush to the wall. He was the only person in the place who happened to be all suited up; that, in itself, was conspicuous. And he had an expression on his face that seemed to say, "Like it or not, I'm in charge from here on out." He annoyed the hell out of Louellen, to tell the truth; every time she glanced up the hall, there he was. She'd have to admit, though, that most of the visitors passing his way were so full of their own worries that they rarely gave him, or his "cot," a second glance.

When, finally, Nell and one of the other daughters led Mr. Farley from the room, Sharon and Louellen entered it for a last checking over. The man from Simpson's followed, unfolding, as he moved, the big zippered bag that had all along been waiting under the cover. Sharon slipped on the toe tag. The rest went swiftly; when he stepped out of the room again, two or three minutes later, the velvet cover was back in place, only now with some bundling underneath, a thickness that might have been folded blankets, or cushions, but no noticeable human shape. The only way Louellen could tell what was under the velvet was by looking twice, staring at the slight bulge and bend made by her frozen left knee, the one they never could get to straighten.

And after that? After the personal effects were gathered, the room was stripped and cleaned, the bed remade, a rose placed on the pillow, and a name card slipped beneath the rose. For a day and a night the room stood empty, as was the custom. Then the rose and the card were sent on to the family. The Farleys mourned, a new family moved in.

Louellen assumed she'd seen the last of the Farleys, but she was surprised only a few weeks later. It happened during a quiet time. Their census was down, and most of the patients were sleeping. Louellen was standing at the desk, busy eavesdropping on two conversations, when Vinnie glanced up suddenly and said, "You see what I'm seeing? Well, I'll be! Look who's here —"

Louellen turned then to see Sharon and Olive speeding down the hall towards Mr. Farley and his daughter Nell. Cora peeked her head out of the supply room, then hurried to join them. The Farleys had been on the unit for so long there wasn't anyone on the staff who hadn't had dealings with them. For her part, Louellen thought she knew whatever could be known about them — especially him. How little that was, she was about to find out.

No one, she decided afterwards, ever knows the all of it.

Mr. Farley was wearing the getup so familiar to Louellen — overalls, plaid shirt, John Deere cap — and walking slowly, slower than she remembered, leaning on Nell's arm. Vinnie stepped away from her desk, and Louellen, too, went forward to meet them. She followed Vinnie. They stood in a sort of receiving line, with Louellen at the tail end.

He didn't look well; he'd been hospitalized, Nell told them. That happened shortly after the funeral. Respiratory problems, long-standing ones. But he wanted to "go back to that place and say hello," Nell told us. "He's kinda lost for communication." And, right then, he was brightening so, smile after smile, at the sight of everyone. One after the other, he received the hugs of Olive, Cora, Sharon, Vinnie.

Hugs were always encouraged at hospice — a way of sharing warmth or filling an empty space. Of speaking — when there are no words for. There are some restrictions, though: don't try if uninvited; not too tightly; never sexy. And there are three recommended forms: the side-to-side, the A-frame, and the full body front-to-front — this last one only if you've been very close. And it's meant to be taken slow and easy.

Hug after hug, all combinations of the three approved forms, and all the while the emotion's building. Louellen's turn was coming up. Louellen didn't think what happened next had anything to do with her personally; it was just the buildup. By the time they were standing face to face, Mr. Farley was still smiling but, Louellen could see it, his eyes were shiny with held-back tears. He started to hug her, side to side, loosely at first, then suddenly went wild, wrenching her — hard — fiercely to his chest, trying to pull all of her to all of him. Louellen couldn't believe what was happening. She let him be for maybe half a minute, then started pulling away, giving signals, a couple pats on the shoulder, quick and light, by way of saying, "there, there. . . ." But he wouldn't quit clutching.

"You come to my house," he wept in her ear. "The flowers are coming out. She isn't there to see them. You come!"

Louellen was so surprised! Shocked, really. She mumbled something about how much "we — all of us" had missed him, how good it was to see him, how they hoped he'd come back to visit again and again. She still doesn't know what else she could have said.

But, by then, Nell had her hand on her father's shoulder, and this last hint, maybe, was the one that registered. Instantly, he let go of Louellen. Drew himself up tall, threw back his shoulders, about-faced, and started on down the hallway, his step unsteady, but determined. As though he knew he was being watched. He had that certain way of carrying himself that had struck Louellen from their first meeting, an almost military straightness. He didn't wave or even once glance back over his shoulder. She thought: he's gotten back his dignity again. And his loss — full measure.

Nola

Suddenly Eva rushed to the altar, grabbed the bread, and threw it into the air. Little pieces of wheat rained on everybody. — Alex Garcia-Rivera

SOMEBODY MUST HAVE THOUGHT Nola Culligan's time was near. With none of her relatives happening to be around right then, and chart time for the nurses, it fell to my lot to help out the priest, Father Martin. "And your name is?" he asked as we set off together. After I told him, he said it again, twice: "Cora. . . . Nice name, Cora." One of the things I'd heard about Father Martin was that he took a great pride in remembering names; it was part of the personal touch he cultivated. Although I'd never spoken to him before this, I'd spotted Father Martin often enough, tearing down the corridor on one errand of mercy or another: this slight, middle-aged man with an energetic stride and a voice with a hidden amplifier in it. I'd rarely seen him in a black suit; he seemed to prefer grays, which wouldn't have been allowed back in the days when I was growing up. He liked to preach on the cleansing power of anger was another thing I'd heard — he was famous for his temper. That was all I knew about him, all secondhand; I'd never seen him at his work.

Right before we entered Nola's room, he warned me: "Watch out for her hands!"

I wondered why, but we were already approaching the bed with Nola in it; that wasn't the moment to ask. I meant to put the question to him after we were done, when we were back out in the hall again, but then he was paged while still in Nola's room. It must have been an urgent call. He packed up his kit at once — and vanished. I never did get a hint of explanation from him. I was left to gather Nola's story in fragments, to fill in the gaps later, on my own, when and where I could.

As it turned out, Father Martin had been low-keyed and somber throughout the rite. He could have carried on perfectly well without me. Finding Nola's hands was the only useful thing I was able to do: they were deeply tangled in the sheets, her fingers oddly bunched. I didn't try to straighten her hands but simply raised up one, then the other, for Father Martin to anoint with holy oil, tracing the sign of the cross on their backs. Nola made no response to any of this. I mumbled a few "Amens" in her stead.

I'm only a volunteer; no one was paging me, or likely to be, so I decided to sit on at Nola's bedside after Father Martin left. Only then did it register: Nola wasn't smiling that day; she hadn't been smiling when we came in, and I'd come to think of her as all smiles.

She was a tiny woman, her skin milk white, unblemished, her hair long and still dark, a bit wild. I never did learn her age, although I assumed it was close to mine — just fewer signs of wear and tear. "A bundle of nerves," her nephew said of her, but that was no longer the case by the time I met her.

After Father Martin had left, I sat on at Nola's side. I didn't say anything, didn't even try. I wasn't in the mood, for a start, and I didn't want to pester Nola with small talk.

The usual question came to me: *Is this all?* More a backwash of feeling than a question, really. I didn't expect an answer. The curtains were open onto the courtyard. I could see the iron gate, and a grassy patch bounded by asphalt. The day seemed stark for so far into spring, the light lusterless, darkened by my mood and my sense of the rite being over too quickly. Too much sacramental efficiency: her little dole of grace given, the patient had been readied for transit, *sealed,* dispatched, without a tremor, an instant of hesitation. Or so it seemed to me.

I had no idea, of course, what Nola was feeling. Her eyes were closed. She'd been struggling to breathe when Father Martin came in and, I have to admit, she did seem easier afterwards. She even stopped breathing a couple of times while I was sitting there. No panic in it at all; it was as if she were practicing a new trick to see if she could carry it off.

That was on Tuesday. Nola didn't die that day, or the day after, or the next. In the meantime, I started asking questions. How long she'd been ill, what sort of person she'd been. I tried not to be too nosy, but I was curious and saw no reason to disguise it. I'd been intrigued by Nola from the first, struck by her — how can I put it? Call it her self-possession, maybe. Something in that smile by way of answer when I asked her how she was feeling, letting me know that I'd asked a question too foolish for words. Since she didn't — or couldn't — speak, every question, every remark I made, echoed back at me and set me to thinking twice. I took advantage of the fact that her nephew spent so much time sitting around, waiting in the alcove outside her room while Nola was being turned, or changed, or left to her sleep. I think it eased him to talk about Nola — he certainly seemed devoted to her. His mother and

Nola had been sisters; both his parents had passed on. Nola was the only one left of that generation.

So — what did I learn? A few things, not a whole lot. "She taught me to skate and to bike. And to swim," he recalled. "See this?" He ran his finger over a scar still visible in the middle of his chin. "Nola didn't believe in training wheels — she started me out on only two, and downhill. She was always mischievous — still partly a child, I guess. Some people called it irresponsibility. I liked to think of it as reckless joy. And kids loved her. I know I did." When the time came, she'd taught him to dance. "And how to drink tequila." He smiled. "You know . . . how to bite the worm to get the vision? '*Eat* the worm,' she urged me. I never could —" He shook his head. "She was mischief, all right . . ."

Somehow Nola had never married, but no one in the family knew the reason; she'd had plenty of admirers and was pretty enough, even now. Pretty — and sweet, too. She'd always been devout, one of the faithful few at mass every morning. In fact, she'd been advised by the nuns who'd been her high school teachers, and later urged by one parish priest after another, to look into a religious vocation, but she'd never taken any steps in that direction. And, here again, she'd never discussed why not. In her nephew's opinion, it was because she liked the world too well. "She had no quarrel with it. She loved life, parties, nice clothes, eating out. Loved to dance. She worked as a tax accountant — and was good at it." I must have looked surprised, I guess we all have our stereotypes: accountant was one of the last things I'd have thought of going with his description of her. "She was really good at it," he went on, "and managed to do plenty of pro bono work at income tax time." He'd been one of her clients ever since he started earning enough to pay taxes. "One of her *paying* clients," he added.

Then this February, he learned that Nola had been dismissed from her job. No explanation, but she didn't seem to be worried and wasn't stressing herself in the search for another. That's when he first began to wonder. There were a few other signs — like temper tantrums. Out of the blue. Flaring up for no reason. She'd do odd things — "embarrassing things" — once stopping in the middle of the street to cup her breasts in her hands. "It wasn't at all funny like her usual mischief," her nephew said. "It was just plain embarrassing."

"But then," he backtracked, "there'd been something we'd not known about. Happened before that —" The family had been summoned by Father Vicente, Nola's parish priest. He didn't want to alarm them, the priest said, but he wasn't going to permit Nola to come to Mass unescorted in the future, not after "the last incident."

"What incident?" — they had no idea.

Had it only happened once, the priest explained, it might have been an accident, but twice had a different meaning. The second time, too, he'd noticed that Nola was smiling. "And she never comes to Confession anymore." This avoidance of Confession seemed to cap it for him; the priest seemed to think that there was some sort of devilment in her.

What Nola had done was to step up for Communion, receive the Host, and flip it into the air. The nephew saw it with his own eyes the first time he escorted her to Mass. On their way over, she'd promised to behave. He'd even asked her if she wouldn't please open her mouth and receive Communion on her tongue in the good old-fashioned way. But, no, that she wasn't willing to do, and she explained why not very reasonably. Said she moved with the times and, anyway, liked to think of herself as an adult, not a baby sparrow. She was so rational about everything, he figured he could trust her.

She seemed to be doing fine as they lined up. When it came her turn to receive, her nephew noticed that her outstretched hands were trembling. With reverence, he assumed. But *then* — he still couldn't get over it — she'd pinched the Host and sent it flying. When it fell to the floor, he felt a wave of shock ripple down the line, the people behind him backing up to make space for the priest to do whatever he had to do to retrieve it. The nephew's next thought was that it had been some kind of spasm, a seizure. Later, he'd changed his mind about that. "A tremble, sure, I'd be willing to excuse. But this —"

This was the third incident. And, whatever the cause, what this said was: Nola couldn't be trusted. A lay minister who visited shut-ins was assigned to bring Communion to Nola at home once a week, and was given instruction about how to guide her hands. Nola never went back to church. "She flicked it," her nephew said. "I know she has a brain tumor and less and less control of her hands, but that was flicking, not fumbling — it was intentional, quite skillful, really, not some kind of crazy reflex. If there's a medical explanation that makes sense, I've yet to hear it. I still don't see how she gets any *thrust*." Here he was — an airplane mechanic by profession — and completely baffled by what he called "the logistics of the thing." He gave a tight little laugh and confessed, "I've even tried flicking coins to get some idea. Of course, coins are so much heavier than wafers —"

I was curious: "Did she ever hint at what she might've meant by a gesture like that — I mean, if she *was* doing it on purpose?"

"Something. . . ." The nephew fingered the scar on his chin. "Something about sharing. And rejoicing — 'not enough joy' in her words — the Eucharist meant to be thanksgiving, celebration, and people forgetting that. Oh, quite a lecture! To tell the truth, I wasn't paying all that much attention — I thought she was simply manufacturing excuses for herself, and — you'll have to excuse my French — right then, I was too pissed off with her to care. It didn't matter what she said."

It was strange. "Not enough joy" was something I'd felt, myself; it was part of my reason for going to Mass so rarely. But, then again, maybe Ken's influence was decisive in my case.

"Anyhow" — the nephew wanted to tell it in sequence — "not long after that monkey business in church came the final straw." One day, when the nephew visited her at home, Nola insisted that he take her place on the sofa, and she settled herself in her new recliner. Then, while carrying on a perfectly lucid conversation about tax shelters, proceeded to relieve herself. Right in front of him! Not a shred of shame! That went way beyond mischief.

And that decided it: something had to be done about Nola. A family council was called, and the first of a long series of visits to doctors began. By the time the diagnosis came, she was having trouble walking. Her vision was blurred. It didn't take a fancy specialist to convince them that Nola had a brain tumor. With the diagnosis, though, came some words they weren't expecting. Inoperable. Terminal. The nephew confessed that he wasn't used to them yet.

That's about as much as I got out of him. Except for the admission that Nola had *always* been "sort of strange."

"You mean something more than high-spirited?" I asked.

"Gosh, I don't know . . . ," he said, "lots of little things we'd gotten used to. . . . Well, wait, here's something, happened way back. I wasn't even born. My mom told me about it, I'd forgotten. Maybe it ties in with this other business — What she did was to catch the garter at my mom's wedding, the one that means *you're next*. Caught it, and tossed it. Nobody'd ever done that before."

Later that afternoon, he approached me to point out an item in the paper. "Seen this?" He was holding the page open, the second page, above the fold.

The headline read: GREGORY PECK READY TO PLAY HIMSELF AND RETIRE, and it went on to say that "after fifty years of playing everybody else, ranging from Dr. Mengele to Atticus Finch, Gregory Peck is ready just to play himself."

I couldn't help laughing, guessing the reason but asking anyway — "Why are you showing me this?" And then we both burst out with the answer at the same moment, it was so obvious. I can't recall the exact words, but the thought was the same: not Nola! Playing anybody else would have been out of the question with Nola. "She was an original," the nephew said, smiling. Then his mood turned wistful. "There won't be another like her," he added, "ever again."

How rare that was in our generation, hers and mine, I thought. I'd been typical: muted, always doing the expected; I never made waves. I'd held my peace even when it wasn't peace. Oh, occasionally, I'd mutter a few words of disagreement, or sulk in silence, but mostly I simply went along, fitting myself into the role assigned me in whatever script I'd been handed. Not Nola. . . . I couldn't help wishing that we'd been able to have a conversation, even once. But that was never to be. It bothered me, her unheard voice, like a letter lost before I'd had a chance to open it.

By Thursday, I knew that Nola didn't have long. She was sleeping most of the time and taking no nourishment. Vinnie asked me to try to give her some liquid if she'd have it. Her tongue, I noticed, was white with thrush. Gently, using a syringe, I coaxed her into swallowing a few cubic centimeters of orange juice mixed with water.

As soon as I started my shift on Friday, I peeked in on Nola.
Still aboard. And she seemed a bit better. She was open-eyed
when I approached the bed. Eye color is not the first thing I notice, but her eyes were such a peculiar shade of blue, almost vi-
olet. I was pretty certain she couldn't see me at that point: her
eyes didn't track when I moved. I think she was still able to
hear, though. She gave me one of her sweetly dazed smiles — a
bit slanting, I noticed, her face seemed somewhat twisted up on
the right side. It wasn't all that striking. You had to look hard
to see that the two sides of her face didn't quite match. Or how,
when she breathed, she'd puff out her left cheek slightly — a
small detail; it didn't seem worth noticing except for what
came after.

I'd made some ridiculous remark about the sun shining and
the birds singing and how good it was to be inside, out of the
heat, and I thought her smile was by way of reply. Then I spotted the orchid. It was deeply purple — no way I could miss it.
Seemed like it was growing out of her hair.

Of course, it was an illusion easily explained: the orchid was
pinned to her pillow and her hair had fanned out surrounding
it. It gave her a drowned-Ophelia look, her hair floating.

Since I had to be out of town that weekend, I stopped by
Nola's room once more before I left on Friday afternoon. The
coma had started an hour or so earlier. Already, the color of her
face was darker. Her whole form appeared flattened, a shell
partly vacated. It was hard to think of her as ever capable of
mischief — let alone sorcery. Drawing closer, I saw her eyelids
flicker, without lifting, as though struggling against weights.

I knew she'd be gone when I got back on Monday, and so it
was. It happened Sunday afternoon; her nephew was at her
side. Her passing was very peaceful, I'm told, and, having no
reason to doubt this, I'm glad for her.

I couldn't go by her door without stepping inside. The room

was still empty. The orchid was gone; in its place, the telltale, silk-petalled rose the nurses place on the pillow after a death. It looked almost real. The curtains were open. The day was hot and brilliant; my eyes burned against the light.

That was weeks ago. Her image still comes to me. When I ask a foolish question, I see her smile. Not only see, but feel my own lips start to stretch until I'm smiling at myself. I'm reminded of her, naturally, in church, and have added her name to those I pray for. I don't go to daily Mass as she did, I don't go every Sunday, not even every holy day of obligation, but I do go every now and then. And, sometimes, when our heads are bowed in prayer, contrition, or boredom, or we're filing down the aisle to receive, scuffing along, eyes fixed on our feet, a sort of sleep comes over me, and a vision — Nola's doing.

I can't blink it away: it's so clear. I see the priest in his stiff vestments paying out Hosts on the altar, like coins on a counter. Hear him chant: "one, one, and one . . ." when, in a flock, the Hosts take to the air, wreathe the tall candles, and soar — Crash to the ceiling, descend . . .

Heads lift. Everything stops, is silent. Astonished, we stand and stare.

As morsels of wheat rain down upon us.

Wedding

WHAT — *here?*"
It takes a while to get used to the idea. In the alcoves, outside the patients' rooms, in the family living room, strangers strike up conversation; most don't know what to think: some are a little shocked; some, unexpectedly pleased, exclaim, "Why *not* here?" All are quickened by the sudden festivity: the ferrying to and fro of wineglasses clinking on trays, the passing finery — the ruffles, flounces, corsages, lace, the twin flower girls clutching their long-handled baskets, skipping down hallways, dropping petals on the linoleum, creating hazard underfoot. One of the flower girls starts twirling, and the other joins in: they call out that the walls are spinning, the floor is spinning — Is no one in charge? They'll have to be stopped.

And where is the bride? The wedding — for the granddaughter of a patient — is to be held in the chapel, the reception in the den. The ceremony is scheduled for two o'clock; it is now two thirty-two.

Nearly a quarter of! They are still waiting. In the meantime, the minister, the bridesmaid, best man, aunts, uncles, cousins, file rapidly in and out of the patient's room. Mrs. Lockhart — patient, grandmother, guest of honor — lies, as she has for so many days, unmoving on the bed that is the centerpiece of the room. She's on oxygen, but not a mask, just sipping through those little straws in her nose. Her hair is nicely brushed, her skin washed and lotioned from her bed bath little over an hour ago, but she wears no makeup or cologne, and no finery, only a clean hospice gown.

Now, as the father of the bride slips quietly into the room, his wife turns to him. "Don't tiptoe in," she scolds. "Don't creep. Maybe she can't see — maybe she can — but she can hear. Let her hear you!"

Does she hear? The father of the bride is doubtful. How can anyone know how much she hears, what she takes in, whether she's aware at all? All anyone can be sure of is that her feet still feel — most painfully — and so must remain uncovered at all times, for even the weight of a sheet is too much, and once caused her to cry out. They are tensed, strangely expressive feet, twisted slightly inwards, towards one another, as if wanting to fold sole to sole, palm to palm, in prayer (although they must not touch); the nails, long and curving back upon themselves, have not been cut in months.

But — aside from pain in her feet, does she feel? The mother and father of the bride have debated this long and heatedly. Are there any other signs? The patient's eyelashes are crusted together, eyes too dry for tears. Only her swollen right arm, now wrapped in a soft towel, now and then exudes a clear fluid.

Her arm weeps, her feet strain to pray, so, yes, the father of the bride concedes, she must feel — *something*. And, once in a great while, her eyes open, a look of bewilderment — or is it wonder? — in them, an almost-speaking gaze, as if to say, *How strange. . . .* These are the only signs.

How quickly everything went downhill after her fall! When she learned of her granddaughter's wedding, Mrs. Lockhart had promised: "I'll be there if I have to come in a wheelchair." No one had expected the wheelchair, much less the bed.

Even so — and this is the crux of the argument — does she still remember that a promise was made? Does she even care? The mother and father of the bride do not see eye to eye on this, and they have been bristling, visibly, for days.

They'd left it to their daughter Janey, the bride — who is also the first and favorite granddaughter — to decide. For Janey, it's never been an issue: the wedding would be wherever her grandmother could come. *Of course,* she still remembers, of course, she still cares — there is no doubt whatever in Janey's mind.

The father of the bride hurries with strong steps out of the room. Only a woman could conceive of a wedding in a place like this. . . . To him, the very idea is an affront to reason, a blot on the whiteness of the day. Joy and sorrow should not mix, or only — if they must — as force against force, one prevailing. What they should have done was postpone the wedding. It's that simple. Let the time of mourning first be over and done.

It baffles him that they were able to get the minister to agree to this. The youth minister, of course, not the senior man. Even so — even a young pastor must know where it is written: "To everything there is a season. . . . A time to weep, and a time to laugh; a time to mourn, and a time to dance. . . ." That's Scripture. That's Holy Writ.

A time — and a place. . . . *Let sorrow keep to its own house!*

The bride has arrived. She wears her veil cast back, her smile radiant. She is milk and honey. She is harvest wheat in white

sun, luminous, bathed in a golden oil. The groom is summoned; he's been roaming, hiding out in the men's room, pacing in the courtyard. Of medium build, sturdy enough, with sleek, dark hair and a strong chin, he is not so much to look at, but he will do. The bride's long dress whispers as she enters the patient's room; the groom shuffles in after her. Beside the bed, the bride speaks a few words, stroking her grandmother's free arm from shoulder to wrist. The grandmother's eyes do not open. The groom stands, shifting from foot to foot; he probes, without pressing, the control buttons that raise and lower the bed. He mumbles — whatever comes to mind. He tells the grandmother how the weatherman got it totally wrong, predicting cloudy all day, yet everything's bright and clear — not a hint of cloud anywhere. As he speaks, the grandmother's hand breaks free of the bride's caresses, rises, rakes the emptiness in front of the groom's face, freezes and hangs in midair. He backsteps, inching away from the bed. The hand returns to rest on the sheet. It's time. Bride and groom take their leave, moving off to their designated places in the vestibule of the chapel.

Cora, minding the phones at the nurses' station, glances up as the bride floats by. She's been reading the monthly log, and the bride's passing, the rustle of the taffeta and tulle, is a welcome distraction, a sight for sore eyes. Only two people have been discharged to home care this week, Cora notices. Other than that, it's the usual list: *Roberto Castilla Admit. — Clyde Oates Disch. H.C. — Celia Hopkins Died. — Hank Watson Disch. H.C. — Abe Stegner Died. — Ruth Blackburn Admit. — Maresa Webb Died. — Chuck Sanders Died. — Denis Long Died. — Agnes Delmita Died. —*

Judging from the number of people milling around the door

to 107, Mrs. Lockhart's bed is about to be launched. Cora scrambles to her feet, and hastens to join them.

The bed wheels have been unlocked, the oxygen hookup transferred from wall unit to a portable canister. Cora and Olive stand at Mrs. Lockhart's bedside, planning beforehand how they will move.

And now Louellen has joined them, drawn, as they've been, by the gathering excitement. Louellen has been none too keen on weddings lately, but this wedding is different — she's at least curious to find out how it will go.

With Louellen lending a hand, Olive and Cora expect no difficulty in navigating the bed. Olive will steer from the head end, Cora and Louellen pushing from the rear. The side rails must go down before passing through doors. They'll reverse in the vestibule and enter the chapel feet first.

Ready?

One more turning —

Once the bed has rounded the corner, everything happens at once. The bed pauses in the vestibule, the bride bends to kiss her grandmother's cheek, the grandmother's eyes open — it happens in a heartbeat — her lips shape the faintest of smiles, her lids close, her smile fades, the bed is swung into reverse, the side rails lowered, it enters the chapel feet-end first; the bed is positioned behind the last pew, angled for a good view of the altar, and the wheels are locked; the side rails are raised; the bride drops her veil, her father moves to her side, the music starts up, the grandmother's breathing grows hoarser, steadily louder — a surf sound, audible to all despite the music.

It is exactly what the father of the bride feared. Confusion reigns. His wife has abandoned the seat reserved for her in the

front pew and stands at the back of the church, holding her mother's hand. Heads swing backward and forward: from the door where the bride stands — a vision — to the bed, to the altar, to the bed, back to the door again.

But his daughter is so lovely, with her graceful neck and up-swept hair, her bright face undimmed, only softened, by the mist of the veil. *How strange* . . . he has known her always, yet can hardly recognize her at this moment.

The bridesmaid has gone forward, and stands now to the side of the main aisle, facing the sanctuary. The flower girls have done what they were supposed to do, more or less on cue, and been whisked aside; a haphazard sprinkling of petals dots the path the bride must travel. The young minister, holding the book open, waits in front of the altar.

Now the bride is nodding to the beat of the music, she is holding out her arm to her father. Now he folds her arm in his. Even the music sounds unfamiliar to him, although they have played it three times, rehearsing their entrance. Can he keep in step? He squints — the light's in his eyes; he's not sure. His heart knocks, and knocks. He's stalled on the threshold —

— So braced and locked, he has to be shaken loose. "Dad?" She nudges. Again, harder. "It's time." She points to her right foot, only the silken toe protruding. Lightly, she taps out the beat: tap, tap, pause (two beats), tap . . . "Remember?" Yes. Now he does. He's starting to move. Free foot, fixed foot. . . . He's moving. Stumbling at first: lifting, then sinking — more plunge than step, it feels. But then the rhythm catches: he steps, and is carried — whether forward or backward, he cannot say; his daughter, stately, beside him, he goes where the music tells him to go: he steps, they step in unison, they do not miss a beat. And now — at last! — the wedding begins.